ACADEMIC

AMBITION

Leigh Jarrett

Published by Steambath Press
An LJ M/M Romance

Paperback published August 2023
ISBN-13: 978-1-998008-14-8

Chapter One | Asher

The words of the form letter stared up at him. Asher had read it over many times while he'd been on the search for a new rooming situation. He still couldn't believe the landlord would leave him stranded like that. He'd been renting the same room from them for the past three and a half years. He liked it there. His room was in the basement away from everyone. His own quiet sanctuary.

The problem was Asher had been there the least amount of time. The other guys renting rooms in the four-bedroom house were working on their master's in computer science degrees. They'd been there longer than him. He was in his fourth year, hoping to graduate with a Bachelor in English he could then use toward getting into a Master's program himself. He wasn't sure what he would do with the English degree but he could figure that out when the time came.

Maybe he was destined to teach.

That possibility made him shiver with anxiety. The thought of standing in front of a bunch of people—the center of attention. It was his worst nightmare. The only time he felt comfortable public speaking was during Spoken Word nights at the coffee shop where he worked. That was different, though. It was a small familiar group in an environment where he felt secure.

From his chair at his desk, Asher looked around his room. Four small boxes were stacked against the wall on one side of the room. It bothered him that they were there. It threw off the balance of his room. He had started packing as soon as he received the letter stating the landlord was moving their son into Asher's room and he would need to vacate it in two months' time.

He'd only left the essentials out anticipating he would relocate as soon as possible to avoid moving during mid-terms. Asher sighed as he smoothed out the wrinkles in the letter. He'd opened and closed it so many times, the creases were soft but set. He'd received the unwelcome correspondence forty-two days ago and he still hadn't found somewhere to move into.

The nearly 0% vacancy rate in Victoria, BC was real.

He carefully folded the letter and tucked it into his notebook. He lifted the colored pencil he'd been using, flipped forward in his notebook a few pages, and continued the shading on a row of panels in the latest manga comic he was drawing: the auburn hair on one of the characters. He drew the darker color down each strand of spikey hair precisely. It had to be perfect.

Not that anyone would ever see it. But the hobby calmed him. Took him out of this world into one of his own creation. He'd been drawing in the Japanese style since he was ten. At the age of sixteen, he changed his style, switching to Yaoi, a form of gay male or boys' love manga.

Of late, the intimate scenes between the characters had become more and more graphic. He'd taken to watching gay porn to get the positioning right. He'd even found a website that let you choose a position by name, then showed you a cascade of videos from porn demonstrating it.

At first, it made him uncomfortable watching and drawing those scenes. His face and ears would flush and his stomach would clench. And other parts of his body would pay attention. Parts he'd prefer not to think about. It took a lot of energy to dismiss and ignore his body's reaction.

He enjoyed the finished product, though. It was real life. Men in a relationship who were having sex with each other. Their cocks pumping. The precum flowing. Their holes on display.

Asher shifted in his chair, anticipating, and switched his colored pencil out for a standard one. His characters were in bed. One character was about to straddle the other. He sketched away filling in the lower half of one of the character's body. A long, thick cock, dripping with desire.

He licked his lips as he moved to the next panel. One character straddled the other. Chest to chest, clinging to each other. Kaito with his hands in Haru's hair. Engaged in a sloppy kiss. Haru's hard cock between them, weeping, as he was seated on Kaito's shaft in the lotus position.

It was Asher's favorite position to draw. It was personal. They were looking into each other's eyes. The next panel had Haru riding Kaito hard. Then the following panel, they were both spilling their seed all over each other. Asher ended the scene with them cuddling afterward.

If he ever had sex, that's the way he would like to see it play out.

Satisfied, Asher tidied up his pencils. He made sure the bottom ends were even before he wrapped an elastic band around them. It was all right for the sharpened ends to be uneven, but the bottoms could not be. He tapped the bundle on the desk to make sure none had moved out of place. Reassured, he tucked the pencils in his desk drawer and closed his notebook.

Asher slipped on his cordless headphones and fired up his new favorite musical playlist on his phone. It wasn't the grunge from the 90s, although he sometimes listened to that. The bands and songs he was interested in were current grunge bands releasing new albums.

He mentally prepared himself. He was hungry but the kitchen would still be occupied. He'd have to brave it to make something to eat for dinner. The headphones helped. It meant he didn't have to speak to anyone. His roommates were nice enough, they just had nothing in common.

It was easier to stay in his own little world while he cooked. He trudged up the stairs as he pressed a control on the side of his phone. He kept the volume on his music low enough that he could hear when someone spoke to him but the headphones acted as a message that he didn't want to talk. He spent most of his time visualizing his next comic as he prepared his food.

Tonight was a quinoa and tofu salad. He'd cooked the quinoa yesterday and placed it in the fridge. Now it was cold, ready to be used. All he had to do was cut up some red peppers, onion, and the medium firm tofu and toss it together with some dressing he kept well stocked.

Asher had been a vegetarian since he was twelve. It had driven his mom crazy, having to request something different be cooked for him. One day, he'd been clicking around on a search engine and stumbled across some videos showing the treatment of animals that were destined to be food. It had turned him off meat. The milk, eggs, and fish were axed later. Now he was vegan.

He liked the way the diet kept him slim. As it was, he was destined to be petite. His body was willowy and he only stood 5'4". He hated the term *twink* but that's what he was. He'd known he was queer ever since he hit puberty. His attraction to males of the species was undeniable.

He pulled out a chopping board, found some space on the counter, and lifted everything out of the fridge. So far his encounters with men had been him simply looking at them. He'd never been in a relationship. He'd kissed a guy last month but that was the extent of his experience. At the age of twenty-four, he was holding out until he made a real connection with someone.

He was a virgin. And he was damned proud of it. The thought of using his body like that, skin to skin with another person, grunting, swearing—sweating. Cumming.

It made him a little queasy.

Everything cut up, Asher tossed all the ingredients into a bowl and added the dressing. He mixed it all together. After he loaded all the dishes he had used into the dishwasher, he headed back downstairs. He preferred to eat in his room. He used the excuse of homework.

He *did* have homework. Two essays were to be written by next week. He was lucky. Words tended to flow easily from his mind. He had a perfect 4.0 grade point average. He decided to sit on his bed and flip open a second personal notebook instead. A half-finished poem was waiting for him. That and a spoken word piece he was hoping to have ready for the next reading event.

Asher decided on the spoken word project. It was post-apocalyptic with the point of view coming from a young girl whose parents hadn't come home from a food pilgrimage.

He scratched away with a pencil, letting the words flow. He preferred to write on paper with a pencil. It felt more authentic than using a computer.

He scooped three mouthfuls of food into his mouth. His phone rang and he had to swallow quickly in order to answer it. He cleared his throat and tapped the answer icon.

"Hello?"

"Hey, is this Asher?"

Asher furrowed his brow. He had no idea who this was.

"Yes. Who is this?"

"I saw your advertisement on the message board at the student union building. Are you still looking for a room to rent?"

Asher straightened up. "Yes. Do you have one?"

"Yeah." The caller chuckled. "I'm in my first year. It wasn't what I expected. Not really my thing. I'm going back home to Ontario."

"You're dropping out?"

"Yup. So my room is going to be empty. The guys need someone to fill it. I told them I'd do them a solid and find someone to take it. Do you want to look at it?"

Asher put his hand on his chest. His heart was drumming hard.

"Is it furnished?"

"Yes. Bed. Desk. Dresser."

Perfect.

"I'll take it."

"Just like that?"

"I just need somewhere to go. I'll make it work." He stroked his hand on the fabric of his tight, black leggings. The excitement had his hands sweating.

"Great! I'll text you the address. I'm moving out on Thursday."

"I'll be there Friday." Asher looked around his room. He could easily pack up the rest of his belongings in three days. He was a minimalist. Most of the packed boxes contained clothes. One of his current roommates had offered his truck to help him move once he found a place.

"What's your last name so I can tell the guys?"

Asher sighed. "Eierkuchen."

"Like *the* Eierkuchens?"

It was bloody embarrassing. People treated him differently when they found out who his family was. They assumed things. Like his life was a free ride. They didn't know he had worked for everything he had accomplished. He paid his own way. Hence simply renting a room.

"Yeah, that's my parents."

"That must be pretty sweet." A long pause. "Why are you renting a room? You could buy a whole house to live in while you go to school."

Asher shrugged even though the guy couldn't see him. "I prefer to pay my own way."

"Huh. Respect."

He wanted off the phone before the guy started asking any more questions about his family's business and their obnoxiously visible wealth.

"Right, so we're good?" Asher asked.

His phone buzzed. He looked at the screen. The guy had sent him the address. He knew the area. It was on a direct bus line to the University of Victoria.

Dammit.

He'd forgotten the most important thing. He was on a strict budget. A lifetime of money not mattering sometimes crept back in. He no longer lived that life.

"I forgot to ask," Asher said. "How much?"

"Nine-fifty a month."

Asher frowned. That was pricey but he could make it work. He would need to pick up more shifts at Café Espresso where he worked as a barista.

"I can do that."

"Good. Then you're set. I'll let the guys take it from here."

"Awesome. Thank you."

"No worries."

The caller disconnected.

Asher ran his hand through his hair, contemplating what his new roommates might be like. Hopefully, they would let him be. He wasn't looking to make new friends.

He leaned forward so he could see his reflection in his floor-length mirror. He tugged at his hair. He'd need to bleach it again soon. His dirty blond hair had started to make an appearance at his root line and throughout the shaved undercut parts on the back and sides. He let the front of his hair fall back over one eye. He wanted to make a good first impression.

Tomorrow before work. He still had some peroxide left. A quick touch-up wouldn't take long. He turned back to his notebook. Windmills. His spoken word essay needed windmills.

Windmills and monsters.

Chapter Two | Shaun

As usual, rugby practice was brutal. Coach had run them through some hard-hitting skirmishes. Shaun knew for certain he'd be covered in bruises and scrapes. His position as full-back meant he had spent the evening bringing down his teammates and grinding them into the turf.

He was glad to pull every sweaty piece of clothing off in the locker room. He groaned as he stretched his muscles out. Even his shins hurt. He looked in the mirror in the bathroom leading to the showers. As expected, bruises were appearing across both shoulders and down his ribs on one side. He'd really feel them and the muscle strain when he woke the next morning.

"Nice work out there, boys."

Coach sounded happy for once. He was usually a bear. Growling and roaring, tearing apart every play they made that wasn't perfect.

"We might actually be ready for the game on Friday." Their captain, Matthew, walked straight out of the showers stark naked, only using a towel to ruffle dry his hair. Shaun huffed out a laugh and went back to soaping his body. Some guys were just plain shameless. Matthew pulled the same shit around the house. No amount of badgering could make him quit putting on a show.

Another of his roommates, Daniel, smacked Shaun's bare ass on the way past.

"Who's up for pizza?" he shouted. A positive response

filled the locker room followed by grunts and chants. Everyone was hyped after practice and feeling good about the upcoming game. They'd been working hard. They had a real chance to make it to the university circuit playoffs.

Shaun dried off, wrapped a towel around his waist, like a respectable human, and made his way to his area of the bench. He dropped his towel and hauled on his underwear, then pulled on his favorite shirt over his head. It was a varsity t-shirt from his high school where he had first discovered his love of rugby. He'd started in his junior year and never looked back. At 6'3" and two-hundred-thirty pounds, the shirt was tight, but he didn't care. It was soft and comfortable.

"You ready?" Matthew nudged Shaun almost knocking him over as he struggled to pull on his jeans. He'd bulked up his thighs again. "Or do you need to check your hair first?"

The question set off a round of laughter. Shaun jammed his feet into his running shoes. "Ha. Ha. Hair's fine." He ran his hands through his short ash-brown strands to make sure they were sitting flat. They'd never leave him alone if he went back to the mirror in the bathroom to check.

Shaun grabbed the felt and leather jacket emblazoned with their team logo off his hook and followed the rest of the guys outside. It was a cold night for March on the West Coast. Drizzly and wet. He snapped the metal buttons shut on his jacket and shivered. Once you weren't running around, the cold air got under your skin. He was glad to pile into Matthew's pickup truck.

They were headed to their usual haunt. A little hole in the wall. The pizza there was fresh and amazing. And the owners weren't afraid of garlic in their sauce. They'd order a medium each and still be hungry after they were done. But they had to watch their carbohydrate intake. There was leftover steak, rare and bloody, in the fridge, they could fill up on once they arrived back home.

They piled into the small restaurant and took up every table in the place but one. The noise level shot from a two to a ten as they all talked over each other. A game of keep-away with the few menus available ensued, which nearly broke out into a wrestling match.

Shaun already knew what he was getting. Meat-lovers. Extra cheese. Heavy on the ground beef. He needed to keep the protein tank fueled. Food was forever on his radar.

He jostled Daniel into spilling his water all over the table.

"Asshole," Daniel responded.

Shaun grinned. "Stop smacking my ass."

"Not my fault you have an ass made for smacking."

Shaun laughed, shoved Daniel again, and joined the chorus of guys all trying to place their orders at once. The owner was used to them. They'd get it sorted. It was probably more business than they'd seen all week. They were yet to get an order wrong despite the chaos.

With the pizzas ordered, the conversation turned to the practice. Pulling apart all the little details. What had been done right—and wrong. Where they could improve. Then smack and strategy talk about the team they were playing on Friday followed.

They had a real chance of winning.

Charlie, the blind-side flanker strolled in through the door. Of course, he wasn't alone. His girlfriend was practically an appendage. A resounding "Boo," rang out. They were only teasing. Jessica, Charlie's girlfriend, was a hoot. One of the guys. She knew her way around rugby better than Shaun did. Her dad had been a coach and she'd played all through high school. Now she played on the women's university rugby team.

She was a force unto herself.

Jessica fell into a seat beside Shaun.

"How's my man Shaun?" she said as she slammed her hand on his shoulder, boisterous like.

Shaun nodded. "He's doing all right."

"Still single?"

Shaun smirked. "Why? Are you offering?"

Jessica scrunched her nose. "Not sure Charlie would be into that."

"Nah, I'm not dating."

Truth was, Shaun hadn't even been on a date in many months. Rugby and school dominated his entire life. Trying to slot someone into his crazy schedule would be cruel. Nothing long-term could flourish in the current insanity that was his life. He wouldn't ask that of anyone.

So for now—no more dating. Once he received his Master of Education in Coaching Studies and nailed down a good job, he would consider opening his world to someone else.

"You sure you're all right?" Jessica asked, quieter this time.

Shaun sighed. "Just tired, I guess."

"Big game on Friday. You ready?"

"I think so."

"You better know so."

"All right. All right." Shaun grinned. "I know so." He leaned back as his pizza was deposited in front of him. Before he had a chance himself, Jessica pulled off a slice and devoured the point. Little crumbles of ground beef dropped onto the table but Jessica chased them up and ate them.

"Go ahead. Help yourself," Shaun teased, then dug into the cheesy goodness. Jessica finished her slice, patted Shaun on the cheek, and went in search of her boyfriend.

Daniel leaned against his shoulder. "She likes you."

And?

"I'm *not* making a play for Jessica."

"Things are rocky between her and Charlie. You never know."

"Even if they split up, I wouldn't be into it. Have you never heard of the bro code? The part where you never date each other's exes?"

"Codes are made to be broken."

Shaun shook his head. "Not interested. She's like a little sister."

"Ew." Daniel pulled back. "Totally backing off then."

"Good." That foray into unrealistic territory averted, Shaun grunted and went back to eating his pizza. By slice seven, he was feeling it. Too much food—too fast. He'd need to walk it off.

He threw some cash down on the table and rose to his feet. It took a bit of maneuvering, but he finally broke free of the crowd of guys filling every available space around him.

"I'm gonna walk home," he said to no one in particular.

Matthew waved at him. "That's a hell of a walk, Shaun. Are you sure you don't want a ride? We'll be leaving in a few minutes."

"If I get tired, I'll call a cab."

Matthew held up a slice of pizza in salute. "Suit yourself."

Shaun strode out into the fresh, cold air. It had stopped raining. The streets were wet but the night sky was clear. In reality, it was going to take him two hours to walk home. He tucked his hands deep into his pockets. The raucous behavior of the evening had worn him out emotionally. He got enough of that at home. Living with two other rugby players was fun but it was also draining. Especially Matthew and Daniel. They were always running on high-octane.

He turned down a street in the general direction of home. If he found himself lost, he could pull up a map app on his phone and get himself back on track. Wandering felt good. He passed by house after house, heritage and modern until he reached a village area with some small shops. An antique store, a thrift store, and a coffee shop under a row of hundred-year-old apartments. The street wasn't well lit and the pitch black made Shaun hustle a little.

He came to a stop when he heard loud voices in the distance. Somewhere around the back of the heritage shops. He was about to ignore it when a voice male and guttural rang out.

"Faggot!"

Then a thump and the sound of someone whimpering.

What the actual fuck?

Shaun ran toward the sound. As he suspected, a group of three men were taking turns kicking a black mass on the wet pavement in the alley. The shape wasn't even definable as human. The black clothes practically disappeared amidst the darkness. Only a shock of white-blond hair sticking out of one end told Shaun that it was a person being beaten on.

"Hey!" Shaun shouted as he raced toward the group. The three guys were slighter than him. It would be a stretch but he had no qualms about taking them all on.

A final kick landed in the middle of the lump of clothing. Shaun could see it was a heavy wool coat. And the person wearing it was groaning and crying.

Shaun grabbed the offending guy and hauled him back.

"Leave them alone!" He wasn't sure yet if the person on the ground was a guy or a girl. Their small size made it impossible to tell. The guy he'd grabbed spun on him.

"Fuck off! This little faggot deserves a beating."

Shaun shoved the guy and he fell back a few steps. "I said leave them alone!" The guy rushed at him and took a swing. Shaun was ready for it. He ducked and tackled the guy to the ground.

The guy's head made a thwacking sound on the pavement. The injury just made the guy spitting mad. Someone hauled on the back of Shaun's coat.

Shaun struggled away from the attempt to pull him off the first guy. He rolled and sprung to his feet of his own volition. "Come on! Pick on someone your own size! Try me!" He held out his arms, using his hands to welcome them to give him a try. The other two guys rushed at him.

The wind was knocked out of Shaun as he slammed against the wall on the opposite side of the alley. A fist landed on his cheek. It startled him. He'd never been hit before.

Rage rose in his chest.

By the time Shaun finished, three men were sporting some fairly serious injuries. They stumbled out of the alley and headed off down the street.

Shaun turned his attention back to the weeping figure curled up on the ground. He kneeled beside them and placed his hand on their back. They flinched and jerked away.

"Hey, you're safe now," Shaun said.

A face emerged from the black clothing. A delicate, beautiful face. There was enough light to make out *his* features. "Where are you hurt?" Shaun asked.

The waif of a guy unfolded himself and rolled until he was seated on the glistening pavement, knees tucked up against his chest. He had a solid bruise forming on his cheek. His face was covered in the remnants of tears. Fresh ones streamed down in rivulets right to his lips.

Shaun was tempted to wipe them away.

"He landed a pretty solid kick." Shaun frowned. "Did it get you in the ribs?"

The guy nodded. "Not just one. My stomach too. And my thigh."

Shaun heaved out a sigh. He was relieved the guy was able to talk. That was a good sign. "We should get you to the hospital. Have them check you out."

The guy shook his head. "I'll go tomorrow. I just want to go home."

"That's not the best decision, considering."

The guy huffed out a breath. "Thank you for fighting those guys off. But I can take it from here. This isn't my first rodeo."

Shaun's eyes grew wide and he placed his hand on the guy's knee. How could someone have a problem with this guy? He was absolutely stunning. He grunted and withdrew his hand.

Maybe that was the problem.

"You've been beaten up before?"

"Last year. Same place." He pointed his thumb over his shoulder. "I work right there. It was my turn to close up tonight. I was headed for the bus stop."

A new curl of rage tangled itself around Shaun's core. The guy was just going about his business. Trying to get home after work. The men who had attacked him were cowards, going after someone who could so obviously *not* defend himself.

"Let me walk you to the bus stop at least."

The guy shrugged. "Okay."

It was a challenge getting the guy to his feet. Even after he was up, it took a few minutes until he could uncurl his upper body. When he did, he was barely taller than Shaun's shoulder.

Shaun kept his hand on the guy's back to steady him.

"Which way is the bus stop?" he asked.

The guy pointed toward the right after the end of the alley.

"Two blocks down."

Shaun wrapped his arm around the guy's back and placed his hand under his armpit, supporting him. "Can you walk?"

"I'll manage." The guy hissed and clutched his side as he took his first step. Each step after that was slow. It took them five minutes to reach the bus stop. The guy slumped onto a bench seat.

"I really think you should go to the hospital." Shaun sat beside him.

"I *really* don't want to go."

"What if you have internal bleeding or something?"

The guy smiled at him. "Yeah? And what if you do? You took a few blows yourself."

"They got off worse than me." Shaun watched the guy's smile turn into a smirk. Then the guy ducked his face away. Shaun was sad to see it go. "Maybe we should both go to the hospital."

The thought of sitting with the guy for hours in the emergency room actually sounded appealing. And he hated the emergency room. But, surely, they could find something to talk about while they waited. He realized he didn't even know his name.

"I'm Shaun by the way."

The guy turned to look at him. There was that smirk again. "Asher."

"Sorry to have met under these circumstances."

"Yeah. Kind of a rescue mission." Asher frowned. "Story of my life."

"Do you get picked on a lot?"

Asher tipped his head to one side and swept his hands down the front of his body. "Look at me. I'm like a neon 'beat me up' sign."

"I don't see that when I look at you."

"Oh, yeah? What do you see?"

Shaun furrowed his brow. How to word this without giving away how beautiful he found Asher. How gentle and innocent he seemed. How he had the sudden urge to protect him.

He tried to be careful with his words.

"I see someone who was just minding their own business. Someone who should be able to take a bus without being harassed." Then he screwed up. "Whose lifestyle isn't harming anyone."

Asher snorted out a laugh. "Lifestyle?"

Shaun closed his eyes.

Jeezus.

Had he actually said that? He knew better. After all the gender study courses he'd taken in university, he knew better. It wasn't a choice. It wasn't a chosen lifestyle.

"I'm sorry," he said. "I didn't mean anything by that."

Asher crossed his arms. "Maybe I'm not even queer."

Shaun's chest tightened. Asher was right. Just because Asher was slight in his build, dressed in a floor-length woolen coat with what looked like a long black skirt beneath—that didn't make him gay. He watched Asher's eyes in the light of a street lamp. They were luscious chocolate brown with thick lashes emphasized by mascara and a solid black liner along the upper lid.

He found himself short of breath.

Asher rose to his feet as the bus cruised down the street toward them. It pulled up fast against the curb, its brakes creaking. The doors flung open and Asher climbed onto the first step with the speed of a snail. He was hurting badly. Shaun wanted to go with him. Patch him up.

Make him tea.

Put him to bed.

Hold him so the world would leave him alone.

Asher gripped the pole and took another step up toward the driver. He fished around in his pocket and presented what looked like a bus pass, then turned to face Shaun one last time.

"Thank you again, Shaun."

The doors of the bus snapped closed and then it was off.

Asher's departure felt as though a vacuum sucked all the air out of Shaun's chest.

Chapter Three | Asher

Asher repositioned himself and tried to get comfortable in bed. He suspected one or more of his ribs might be broken. He probably *was* going to have to go to the hospital. He hated doing that whenever someone roughed him up. It was embarrassing.

He'd lied to the guy who helped him. It hadn't been a year since the last time someone had taken their fists to him. It was more like a couple of months. Usually, it wasn't a full-on beat down like he'd experienced last night, but he'd taken a few knocks throughout his life.

He sighed and stared up at the ceiling. The pain medication he'd tossed back was barely taking the edge off. The thought of going back out into the cold to catch the bus to the hospital was enough to keep him in place. He should've taken the guy, Shaun, up on his offer of going to the emergency room with him. The thought of sitting with Shaun for hours on end wasn't unpleasant.

Even though he had jock written all over him.

Shaun had dispensed with his attackers like someone who was used to aggression. Contact sport. Asher had hidden his face throughout but the sounds had painted a pretty vivid picture. Plus, Shaun's knuckles had been bruised and bleeding when he finally crouched down at his side.

Asher sighed. He'd had kind grey eyes, Shaun. So much concern with a hint of rage burning behind them. Shaun wouldn't have given up until Asher was safe. That much he knew.

His roommates were going to be horrified. He touched the tender bruise on his cheek. Despite his best efforts to keep to himself, his roommates had come to care about him. One look at him over breakfast and they'd be threatening to find the guys and kill them for him.

The thought made him smile. Their geeky, soft bodies wouldn't stand a chance. But he would appreciate the sentiment. He was going to miss them.

He rolled and looked at his phone. 6:52 am. Too early to get up. He didn't have class until 2. And he didn't have to attend in person. He could retrieve the notes and assignments from the university website. If he could find a comfortable position, he could stay in bed until the other guys were up. Getting a ride to the hospital sounded infinitely better than bussing.

The next time he looked at his phone, it was almost 9. He could hear people moving around upstairs. Thursday was an easy day for all of them. He swung his feet off his bed— slowly. His whole body ached. His gaze fell on the additional boxes he had packed yesterday. He was almost ready to move. Just his textbooks, notebooks, sheets and remaining towels needed to be boxed up.

He rose to his feet and groaned. It was a struggle to stand up straight. He stepped closer to the floor-length mirror and lifted the edge of the black, grunge-band t-shirt he was wearing. Blotches of purple and crimson bruising marred his abdomen and ribs. He hissed as he touched one of them.

Asher let his shirt fall back in place and stepped closer to the mirror to examine his face. His eye above the bruise on his cheek was bloodshot. One guy had caught him off guard. He'd been punched in the face before he had a chance to play turtle on the ground.

Thankfully, the skin on his face hadn't split. He attempted a deep breath. It was debatable if he needed to go to the hospital.

He remembered the concern shadowing Shaun's eyes when he had refused to go.

Asher sighed. He would do it for Shaun even though he would probably never see the guy again in his life. He pulled on a pair of black harem pants and headed for the stairs.

As expected, the guys were visibly upset.

"What the hell happened to you?" Darren was the first to speak, joined by a chorus of "What the fuck!" and "Who did this to you?" Lucky him … all three of his roommates were home.

"Some homophobes caught up with me outside the coffee shop."

Asher wandered over to the coffee pot. There was fresh coffee. He prayed it would help revive him. He was emotionally exhausted by last night's experience.

"Just some random guys?" Darren again.

"Wrong place. Wrong time," Asher said. "They had an issue with my clothing choices."

William, the other roommate who shared the basement with Asher, shook his head. "I don't know why you do it. The way you dress, you risk your life every time you leave the house."

Asher scowled. "I don't dress to please other people."

His third roommate, Eric, approached Asher and placed his hand on Asher's shoulder. "How bad is it? I can take you to get checked out if you'd like."

"Thanks, Eric. Let me get a coffee in first, though. Okay?"

"Yeah, it'll be a long day waiting around."

Asher drank the coffee but decided against breakfast. He tucked a protein bar into his black over-shoulder bag along with a notebook and some pencils.

As expected, after Asher was triaged, it took another 5 hours before he saw a doctor. Then a CT scan and an ultrasound and more waiting. In total, he was there for over 7 hours.

By the time he exited the emergency department, it was dark. Asher shivered each time the outer doors of the hospital automatic entry opened. He had parked himself between the two sets of doors as he waited for Eric to pick him up. The black woolen leggings, floor-length skirt, turtle neck sweater, and heavy black boots were barely doing the job of keeping him warm.

He hustled and slid into the passenger seat of the Mini when Eric arrived.

"So, what's the verdict?" Eric asked.

"I'm going to be sore for a while. But nothing is broken or damaged."

"That's a relief." Eric pulled away from the pick-up area and headed for Bay Street. "So, you're moving tomorrow. My offer still stands to help you out."

"Thanks. I'm going to take you up on that. What does your day look like for time?"

"I've got all afternoon for you."

"Can we do 3?"

"Sure. Will someone be there?"

Asher shook his head. "No. One of the guys—Matthew texted me where to find a hidden key. They're all out doing something. Some game or something."

"Playing or watching?"

Asher shrugged. "Not sure."

Eric frowned. "They better be nice to you."

"I don't have any other options." Asher smiled. "Can't be

any worse than you guys."

Eric snorted out a laugh and turned into the driveway of their house. Asher was cautious as he ascended the stairs to the front door. Every step he took hurt. He thanked Eric for giving him a ride to and from the hospital, then headed down to his room.

A wash of relief cascaded over him as he pressed the door of his bedroom closed behind him. He would wait until the kitchen cleared out before he went up to make food. He didn't feel like fielding any more questions. Eric would fill the others in on what the doctor had said about him.

He grabbed a notebook and a roll of pencils and propped himself up at the head of his bed. He used piles of pillows to support himself on every side. He opened the notebook.

He had a page of seven panels of various sizes. Kaito and Haru were at a house party and they had snuck off to make out in the shadows of a back porch. No words were spoken.

Asher added quote squares of sounds. Ah! Wah! And Uh! The following panel had Haru's internal thoughts. Haru admitted to himself that he was in love with Kaito.

Asher closed his eyes. To be in love. He longed for that feeling. Where another person would haunt your every thought; a man who you'd be desperate to spend every moment with.

He sighed. It was a dream. One he didn't see ever being fulfilled. He didn't meet that many people and he tended to stay to himself. Plus, he was unusual. A delicate, feminine gothic kind of guy who was obsessed with drawing, writing, and living inside his head. Then there was his OCD.

That was enough to drive anyone crazy.

Kaito and Haru headed to Kaito's and had sex. Missionary position. SLCH, SLP, THWP. AAH! HFF! AGH! Coming!

Kaito filled Haro's ass and Haro spilled onto his own stomach.

Asher swallowed as his cock hardened. He touched the front of his skirt and brushed his thumb along his stiff shaft. It wasn't often he touched it. He wasn't even sure what he thought about its existence, but the urge overtook him. He shuffled down in bed, found his way up under his skirt with both hands, and shoved his thick, woolen leggings and underwear down past his hips.

He groaned as he encased his cock in one hand. His strokes were slow and easy. He bent his knees and dug his heels into the bedding, and undulated up into his fist.

Shaun's eyes flashed through his mind.

The image caught him by surprise. He'd never had any success picturing someone when he touched himself. He fixed Shaun's face in his lust-fueled fantasy. Shaun had a strong jaw, high cheekbones, and full lips. His expression had been stern. Asher suspected that was a constant state for Shaun. He imagined Shaun gazing up at him from his knees.

Fuck.

Shaun licked his lips and descended onto Asher's cock with his mouth.

Double fuck.

Asher scrambled to reach his bedside table with one hand and grabbed a wad of facial tissue. He capped the soft square sheets of it over the head of his cock. A few more pumps on his shaft and he erupted into the meager protection against soiling his clothes. Every jerk made him feel lightheaded. His heart thudded in his ears. It took incredible effort to stay quiet.

Then it was over.

His face flushed with splotches of red. His ears prickled as embarrassment and a hint of remorse crawled along under his skin as his body stilled.

He shuddered and sucked in a breath. Tears streaked down his cheeks. He wasn't sure where the aversion had come from. He had a complicated relationship with his cock. He remembered being horrified when he hit puberty and it started to grow. But he had enjoyed touching it. Then he'd taken his playtime to the point where he had ejaculated. He remembered staring down at the mess on his hand and vowing to never do that again.

Asher cleaned his cap with the tissue and pitched the crumpled, sticky mess into the garbage can beside his bed. Of course, he *had* done it again—played with his cock. He tried to keep it to a minimum. It was a reminder that he lived in a male body.

His notebook had fallen to one side and his pencils had rolled onto the floor. He hadn't even noticed, he had been so absorbed by the image of Shaun sucking him off.

He closed his eyes. He could sleep.

Thankfully, Eric took it upon himself to load all of Asher's boxes into his truck. There was no way Asher would have been able to lift and carry anything. He would be hurting for a long while still.

It only took them twenty minutes to drive to what would be Asher's new home. He'd done the street view on a map app to see what the house looked like. It was an older heritage home, the siding painted a cream color with black shutters. Asher recognized it immediately.

He pointed it out to Eric.

"There it is."

"Nice."

Eric parked on the road in front of the house. There was a gravel driveway that extended down the left side of the house with an old carriage house at the end. There were already two cars parked there. The remaining drive was not enough space for Eric's truck.

Asher headed for the gate to the right side of the house. It opened onto a pathway lined by what he assumed would be flowering plants. It had that feel. Like an English garden. He could see the start of a patio area at the back of the house. He scanned the ground to the side of the path. He was looking for a flat stone with a sunflower painted on it.

"You find it?" Eric leaned over where Asher was looking.

Asher pushed some shrubbery aside. Beneath it lay the stone he was looking for. He lifted the stone and thankfully, the key was there. He brushed the dirt off the jagged silver metal.

"Let's find my room first. Then we can load in my stuff."

Eric let Asher lead the way. Asher grasped the handrail of the stairs. They appeared to be new; painted cream like the house. The front door was painted black like the shutters. The color; Asher felt as though the house was welcoming him. He unlocked the door.

The first thing he noticed was the floor. Solid planks stained a warm brown that extended from the front door past the staircase to a door at the end of the entryway. Asher assumed the kitchen would be back there. The walls were a deep burgundy.

It had a homey feel.

"Do you know where your room is?" Eric asked.

Asher shook his head. "No, the guy Matthew didn't tell me." He looked up the stairs. "Let's try up there." He led the way. The ascent was brutal on his ribs.

He opened the first door they came to.

He covered his nose.

Oh my god.

The scent of sweat and mildew assaulted him. And the room looked like it had been tossed by burglars. Clothes, books, and a tumble of sheets trying to escape the bed they should have been on. It was almost impossible to see the floor.

Asher shut the door.

"Okay. Not that one."

He walked down the hall and opened another door. It was the bathroom. Again, it looked like it had been tossed. The floor was covered in towels and the counter was awash in a collection of disorganized deodorants, razors, toothbrushes, and toothpaste. Three kinds of everything. Also occupying the space. A tub of hair gel. A nose trimmer. Two combs and a brush.

Asher walked in and opened the window by the toilet. The room needed a good airing out. It smelled of humidity. He shook his head with disbelief as he passed an empty laundry hamper.

The room next to the bathroom was somewhat neater than the first one he had encountered. At least the clothes were in the closet. This one had posters plastering the walls. Rugby players by the looks of it. Asher nodded. That's what Matthew had said. They were at a rugby game tonight.

He closed the door and tried the last room on the landing. It was like walking into a different house. The bed was even made. And someone had attempted to battle the odor of sweaty bodies that seemed to be permeating the air upstairs.

"Not up here," Asher said.

"Basement?"

"I don't know." Asher ambled down the stairs and looked for the basement door. He found it in the kitchen. He opened it and peered down into the dark depths. There was a rickety set of stairs. A light at the bottom with a pull chain. No sheetrock. Open studs.

God, I hope not.

"Over here," Eric called. He stood by another door off the kitchen. He'd flung it open. Inside a plain room, devoid of belongings. A bed with a bare mattress, worn headboard, an adequate desk, and an antique tallboy dresser. The closet was closed off by a curtain.

Asher groaned. The days of having a quiet, secluded space to retire to were over. A room right off the kitchen was going to be noisy. He hoped his roommates weren't big cookers.

"I'll go bring in your stuff," Eric said.

Asher offered him a weak smile. "Thanks, Eric."

It took Eric less than thirty minutes to load all of Asher's boxes into his new room. He sat on the bed and stared at them after seeing Eric out and thanking him again. He retrieved a knife from the kitchen and popped open the first box full of clothes. He had carefully labeled everything. He was going to start with clothes so he could shift the majority of the boxes. There was a back hallway off the kitchen where he could store the broken-down cardboard.

He hung what clothes needed to be in the closet and put the rest of the folded clothes into the dresser. He had a whole box of shoes and boots. They filled the entire floor space in the closet.

Above the desk was a shelf. It looked sturdy enough to hold all his textbooks. He tested the theory and the shelf held. He set his laptop on the desk and filled the top drawer with all his office-type supplies. Pens, paperclips, a stapler, sticky notes, and his bundles of pencils. He tucked his notebooks into the second drawer of the desk.

The bed only took a few minutes to make. Bottom, top

sheet, and pillows. And a comforter that took up an entire box by itself. Except for one item. He reached into the bottom of the box and lifted out the teddy bear he'd had since he was a baby. It was ragged and well-loved. Worn brown patchy fur. A blue jacket and a floppy black hat. He placed it in front of the pillows.

Asher looked around the room. It felt new to him—but comfortable. The room had wainscot on the lower half of the walls. Cream colored like the exterior. The walls above were a dark forest green. The darker color suited Asher. It made him feel secure. Like a warm hug.

He pulled a throw blanket out of the last box and stretched out on the bed. It was pleasant enough. A newer mattress with a memory foam topper.

He hauled a pillow under his head, tucked his teddy against his chest, and pulled the throw blanket over his shoulders. That's the last thing he remembered for hours.

Asher was startled awake by thudding, laughter, and loud voices all talking at once. Then the clatter of pots and running water joined in.

"Did you see that?" someone shouted. "I took him *down*!"

"Rattled his cage for the rest of the game!"

"We dominated the field!"

Then the sound of what could be only described as dogs woofing. Followed by the chanting of a name Asher assumed was a sports team.

"Oh, shit," someone said after an attempt of shushing. "The new guy is probably here."

"Crap. He's going to think we're animals."

Exuberant laughter and the assigning of certain animals to what Asher had figured out were three stereotypical jocks. A pig, an ox, and a bulldog were the final tally.

A knock on Asher's door had him scrambling. He whipped off the throw blanket and stuffed his teddy under his pillow. "Come in."

A friendly face appeared in the open doorway. Dark curly hair. A handsome face with mischievous brown eyes. "I'm assuming you're Asher."

"That would be me."

"I'm Matthew. I texted you." He smiled. "Sorry about the ruckus. We won our game."

"Rugby, right?"

Another face appeared in the doorway. "That's right." This guy was tanned with blond hair. He had it tied back in a knot at the back of his head. Asher's heart fluttered a little. Gorgeous. He had intense green eyes and lips made for kissing. "I'm Daniel."

Asher swallowed. "Nice to meet you both."

Matthew hitched a thumb over his shoulder. "Come join us in the kitchen. We're going to make something to eat. Our other roommate had to make a run for the john."

Asher felt like he didn't have a choice. It would be unfriendly to turn them down. He wouldn't be making a habit of it but for today he could join them.

He followed them out into the kitchen and took a seat at the 50s-era Formica and metal table. The guys had Styrofoam trays with visible slabs of red meat in them on the counter.

Of course, they were meat eaters.

Matthew retrieved a massive cast iron frying pan from under the oven, placed it on an element, and turned on the heat. He turned and faced Asher. He tapped his cheek.

"What happened to your face?" he asked Asher.

"I had a difference of opinion with someone."

Daniel chuckled, leaned against the counter, and crossed his arms. "No offense, but you're kind of small to be picking fights with anyone."

A deep voice from the kitchen doorway startled Asher.

"He didn't."

Asher turned in his seat.

Oh, my god.

Shaun.

His stomach trembled and twisted.

The guy he had jerked off to last night—standing not even two feet from him. He had a black eye and a row of butterfly bandages keeping a cut on his cheek stitched together.

"Shaun," Asher whispered.

"You two know each other?" Matthew asked.

Daniel pointed at Asher. "He's the guy ... the guy you saved the other night." He laughed. "The guy whose fault it is your face is so messed up."

Asher rose to his feet. "That was my fault?"

Shaun walked into the room. "Not your fault. You weren't doing anything wrong."

Asher sat back down. This couldn't be happening. He was going to be living in the same house as the guy whose eyes he'd memorized. Shaun was over at the counter, fussing with the bloody pieces of flesh. Asher hadn't realized Shaun's face had taken such a beating, he'd been so focused on his eyes. The blackening around his eye must have appeared later. He furrowed his brow. It *had* looked red and swollen along his one brow. He hadn't been paying much attention.

The image of Shaun's face that Asher had burned into his mind didn't include the injuries.

Shaun turned to face him. "Did you go to the hospital?"

"Yesterday."

"You all right?"

"Just a bit of bruising."

Shaun nodded. "Good." Then he went back to preparing the steaks. Daniel loaded a truckload of cut broccoli into a steamer poised over the top of a boiling pot of water.

Asher's stomach rolled as the smell of the cooking steaks filled the kitchen. They were barely left on the heat for more than a few minutes a side.

Plates clattered onto the counter.

Four.

"Ah, no ...." Asher jumped to his feet. "I don't eat meat."

"Of course, you don't," Daniel said.

Shaun smacked Daniel's shoulder with the back of his hand. "Shut it!" He looked over his shoulder at Asher. "Do you want some broccoli?"

Asher's stomach growled. He'd missed dinner. He'd been focused on unpacking. He knew there was a grocery store within walking distance from the house but he hadn't gotten that far with his move-in. He'd head there tomorrow and stock up. He hadn't brought much with him. Just some ramen noodles, oatmeal, a bag of quinoa, and a container of uncooked rice.

"Yes, please. Just salt ... no butter."

Daniel made a scoffing noise.

Asher put his heels on the rungs of the chair, tucked his knees close to his chest, and crossed his arms. If he could disappear, he would. Daniel had already taken a dislike to him.

"I swear to God, Daniel," Shaun said. "I'll knock you out."

"You gonna keep saving him?" Daniel asked and shoved Shaun aside.

Shaun lifted a large serving of broccoli onto a plate. "Just fucking cut it out." He crossed the kitchen and set the plate in front of Asher with a fork. "There's salt on the sideboard."

"Thank you," Asher whispered.

The table jostled as three muscular men dumped their plates onto its surface and dropped into their seats. The bile rose in Asher's throat. He had to close his eyes. The slabs of flesh were floating in pools of blood, offset like a horrific murder scene on white plates.

Asher gagged and covered his mouth. The smell was overwhelming. He shoved his chair back and made a run for his bedroom. He was followed by the sound of Daniel laughing. He slammed his door and sank onto his bed. Two fat tears rolled down his cheeks.

An argument erupted in the kitchen. Hollering and a scuffle. Chairs screeching. They were fighting about him. Shaun was defending him. Daniel was being an asshole.

Matthew was trying to break things up.

He wanted to go home.

Asher shuddered through a sob. Except this was it. This was his home now. Unless someone else answered his ad on the message board at the university. He could pray for that to happen.

Alternatively, the guy who had phoned was right. He could ask his parents to buy him a house. Then he wouldn't have to put up with ignorant jocks or anyone else. He would have the place to himself. Thousands of square feet to rattle around in on his own. Maybe even a pool.

He covered his face with both hands and took a deep breath. He had promised himself he wouldn't fall back on his family's money. It was the easy way out.

Asher lay back and curled himself up on his bed. He reached under his pillow and retrieved his teddy bear. He held it to his chin. The kitchen grew silent after a clatter of dishes.

Someone knocked on his door.

"Asher … can I come in?"

Asher recognized Shaun's voice. He contemplated ignoring Shaun until he went away. His kind eyes, though. He knew they would make him feel better.

"Yes."

Shaun opened the door and closed it behind him. He pulled out the chair from under Asher's desktop and sat down. "I'm really sorry about that."

There they were. The gentle eyes that made him feel better, gazing down at him.

"Not your fault."

"Daniel's a prick." Shaun clasped his hands together, leaned forward, and rested his elbows on his knees. "Pretty face, but a nasty attitude when he doesn't understand something."

That didn't sit right with Asher. His stomach clenched.

"I'm not a something."

"Something extends to people too."

"I didn't do anything to him."

"No, you didn't … other than confuse him."

"What's so confusing? I'm a human being."

"I know that. Matthew knows that. Daniel will come around."

Asher sighed. Two out of three was somewhere to start, at least. He tucked his knees up tighter to his body. He still didn't feel safe but Shaun's presence was helping.

"Who's that?" Shaun pointed at Asher's stuffed bear. He'd forgotten he was still clutching it.

"Stanley." Asher stuffed his childhood toy under his pillow.

"Does he make you feel better?"

"Sometimes."

"Cool. Hey, your broccoli ended up on the floor. Are you

still hungry?" Shaun reached forward and touched Asher's shoulder. An ache of comfort flowed through Asher's body.

Shaun hadn't laughed at him or belittled him for having a comfort toy. He had asked *who* is that? Like it was perfectly normal. Not *what* is that? He'd accepted it and moved on. Like it was something every adult in the world did—which they didn't.

"I can make something later."

Shaun rose to his feet. "Let me make it for you. Are you a ramen guy? I don't have to put in the flavor packet. I think we only have chicken."

Asher released a long breath. "That would be perfect." He *was* hungry.

"On it." Shaun headed out to the kitchen. A rush of water flowed into a pot and then a burner clicked on. Asher stayed on the bed. It wasn't until he heard the water boiling that he ventured to his door. He looked into the kitchen. The only person there was Shaun. He was standing in front of the stove, a pair of chopsticks in his hands, poking at the noodles cooking in the water.

The light over the stove was the only illumination. The rest of the kitchen was dark. It felt comfortable and warm. Shaun's presence as he cooked food for him had Asher relaxing.

"Do you want some tea?" Shaun asked.

"Do you have green tea?"

Shaun set the chopsticks on the counter and opened the cabinet next to the range hood. "I think we might, actually." He dug around, then reached to the back of the cupboard. A box of green tea was in his grasp as he pulled his hand back. "I'll put the kettle on."

It was sweet, Shaun wanting to take care of him but he could make his own tea.

"I can do it." Asher lifted the kettle off the stove top and filled it up at the sink. Shaun stepped up beside him with the pot poised to drain the noodles.

"I'm assuming you don't want the water without any broth."

"Yeah, just the noodles are fine."

Shaun's shoulder rubbed against Asher's. Asher enjoyed it for a brief moment, then walked over to the stove to start the kettle. The contact had made him feel fuzzy inside.

"Cups?"

Shaun pointed to a cupboard as he retrieved a bowl and dumped the noodles into it. "We have some sweet chili sauce if you're looking for a bit of flavor with this. Pretty sure it's vegetarian."

"I'm vegan. But, yeah, if you don't have any soy sauce, I'd like some."

"No soy sauce here." Shaun pulled open the fridge, grabbed the sauce, and placed it on the table. "So, what's the difference? Between vegetarian and vegan."

"I don't eat milk, eggs, or fish either."

"Not ever?"

Asher tipped his head, studying Shaun. He really *was* interested. Shaun pulled out a chair and sat down across from where he'd placed Asher's bowl.

"I've been known to eat sushi on occasion," Asher replied as he fussed with a tea bag. He placed it in his cup and set it beside the stove to wait for the kettle to boil.

Asher slid into his seat. He appreciated that Shaun had given him chopsticks. Asher was a purest. Asian food should be eaten with the proper utensils.

He checked the label on the chili sauce. No fish sauce. He dumped a heap of the sauce onto the noodles. He'd make a cultural exception with the addition of a little flavor.

"I've never had sushi. Kind of a meat and pizza crowd around here." Shaun waited until he caught Asher's eye. "Maybe you could take me sometime … for sushi."

A flush rose in Asher's cheeks. He covered up by stuffing a heap of noodles into his mouth. The chili sauce had just the right amount of heat. His stomach would have started to feel better if Shaun hadn't asked him to share a meal. Why had he asked him to do that?

He slurped up the noodles hanging off his bottom lip and chewed them. The best he could manage was a nod until after he swallowed.

"Sure." Asher moved the noodles around in his bowl. "We could do that."

He had no intention of ever taking Shaun out for sushi. It was his first night with new roommates. He had planned to be as agreeable as possible.

Until he'd run out of the room, disgusted by their choice of sustenance.

It seemed Shaun had read his mind.

"Sorry about the steak. I'll give you a heads up next time we're going to cook any."

"I appreciate that. I'll try to be out." Asher snagged some noodles. "I can't stand the smell."

"Maybe we could use the barbeque. Keep the smell out of your room."

Even better.

"Thank you."

Asher looked up from his noodles. Shaun was staring at him.

"Those guys the other night had an issue with your clothes?" Shaun asked.

"Amongst other things."

Shaun watched Asher in silence, then swallowed hard, making his Adam's apple bob. "I like the way you dress."

Asher's eyebrows rose. "Even the skirt?"

Shaun pursed his lips, then relaxed them. "It suits you."

That was quite a surprise. Most straight guys had negative or ignorant things to say about his choices in fashion. He had never had one say they *liked* it. Shaun appeared to be a complicated guy. How complicated, he wasn't sure. It might be interesting to find out. He was certainly intrigued. He decided to open up. To see how far Shaun's acceptance of him would carry.

Asher set his chopsticks down.

"I am gay by the way. You were right."

Shaun leaned back. "I didn't mean to assume."

"I don't exactly hide it. My voice and my little mannerisms usually give it away. Plus, God decided to give me this body and face. Don't really have much of choice but to be *out*."

Shaun scowled. "What's wrong with your face? I like your face."

Asher's ears started to burn. He cleared his throat. "Nothing, I guess."

The conversation was talking all sorts of bizarre twists and turns. Shaun was confusing him. He didn't like to be confused. He liked everything all lined up and predictable.

I like your face.

What did that even mean? Was Shaun attracted to him or did he simply appreciate how feminine Asher's face was? The former gave him all sorts of butterflies. The latter made him sad. It was always going to be an issue. His whole life to date had been dictated by his face.

When he was a teenager and he'd let his hair grow long, Asher had frequently been mistaken for a woman. Using the washroom for his gender assigned at birth often led to men staring at him like he was in the wrong place. Some even verbalized it.

He had started to use the women's washroom until after he cut his hair and changed his style to be somewhat more masculine. Then he'd swung back during his first year of university.

He'd been battling the walk down the thin edge of a knife for his entire life. Never knowing for sure what side of the blade he was supposed to land on—which side he wanted to land on.

He must have been scowling.

He'd certainly stopped shoveling the food into his mouth.

"Are you all right?" Shaun asked.

Asher looked up into Shaun's eyes. They really did make him feel better.

"Just thinking," he replied.

"Did I overstep?"

Asher shook his head. "Just not used to straight guys saying anything positive about my face." Girls on the other hand had been fawning over him since high school. He had come out in his junior year and had immediately attracted a female following. The guys weren't as kind.

Shaun scrubbed his hand across his lips. "You know ... not all straight guys are the same."

"I'm finding that out." Asher smirked. "Thank you ... for everything."

"Is there anything else I can help you with?"

Asher rose from his seat. He'd only eaten half the noodles but he felt full. His stomach was so full of flutters and jumps, that there wasn't much room for food.

"I'm good." Asher scraped his bowl into the garbage and

rinsed out the bowl. There was no dishwasher but the sink had a sponge and dish soap at the ready.

"If you need anything else, give me a shout." Shaun left the table and headed for the doorway into the kitchen. "I'm the bedroom at the end of the hall."

Asher smiled and looked over his shoulder. "The tidy one." He blushed as Shaun's face lit up with a grin. "I was looking for my room. Stumbled across some atrocities."

"I don't know how Daniel can stand it."

"That's his room? The one that looks like a dump?"

Shaun laughed. "That would be his."

"Doesn't match his looks."

"Matches his attitude to a fault, though."

Good to know. Asher turned back to the sink and started washing his bowl. He was used to running into ignorant guys but he'd never lived with one.

"Good night," Shaun called out as he headed for the stairs.

"See ya," Asher whispered into the air. Shaun had already jogged halfway up the stairs by the time Asher had his turn to speak. He finished his dishes and retreated to his room with his tea.

As he lay in bed, his mind turned to Shaun's eyes and the kindness he had shown him, both in rescuing him outside the coffee shop to defending him in the kitchen.

He fell asleep to the image of Shaun cooking noodles for him.

Chapter Four | Shaun

Shaun closed his bedroom door, leaned against it, and slid to the floor, his back against the wooden barrier that would give him the privacy he needed to have a meltdown.

He bent his knees, placed his elbows on them, and covered his face with his hands. He was sweating and quivering. He'd barely been able to hold it together.

Never. He had never been so nervous to talk to someone. It had been different outside the coffee shop. Asher had been a random guy who needed help. Even then, Asher's presence had set off all sorts of alarm bells. Bells he had never heard before when it came to a guy.

Walking into that kitchen and seeing Asher there had nearly caused him to become mute. He'd only been able to speak because it was in Asher's defense. He'd nearly run after Asher when he leaped up from the table. But he hadn't—he'd had a few things he needed to say to Daniel.

It was cruel and uncalled for; Daniel laughing at Asher's discomfort. They had no way of knowing why Asher had decided to become vegan. Maybe there was trauma associated.

He just wanted Asher to feel at home.

Then for some insane reason, he'd offered to cook Asher noodles. Shaun hadn't been able to leave the kitchen and head to bed. He had needed to make sure Asher was all right.

Shaun groaned. Sitting there with Asher, he had said all sorts of stupid things.

I like the way you dress.
I like your face.
Maybe you could take me for sushi.

What the hell had he been thinking? Truth and desire had spilled out of him like he had known Asher for years. That they were friends. Shaun rubbed his face with his palms and pressed the heels of his hands against his eyes, trying to drown out the thoughts swirling around in his head.

More than friends.

He wanted to be so much more than friends.

The realization stunned him. There had been several guys in the past whom he had found attractive, who churned up his insides a little, but nothing like this.

He wanted to gather Asher up in his arms. Asher and his teddy bear—and hold him. Kiss the back of Asher's neck and tell him he was safe; that everything was going to be all right.

Shaun pulled out his phone and stared at the empty search field on his browser. His fingers went to work. *How do I know if I'm bisexual?*

There were a lot of results. Shaun focused on one that was an online test.

How do you react when you see an attractive person of the same gender?

C. I sometimes feel a bit attracted.

When you see yourself in a romantic relationship, who do you see yourself with?

That was a hard one. Right now, it was Asher.

D. Mostly with someone of the opposite gender, but sometimes with the same gender.

Have you ever had a crush on a friend of the same gender?

Shaun's thumb hovered above his screen. He'd had a best friend in high school who made his stomach all squirrely when he stood or sat too close to him.

B. I've thought about it, but it hasn't gone beyond that.

How comfortable are you with the idea of being in a sexual situation with someone of the same gender?

Shaun drew in a long breath and released it. He pictured Asher. He'd like to see all those black clothes in a pool on the floor at Asher's feet. Asher stretched out on the bed in the nude—his cock hard, begging for attention from Shaun with his eyes.

His cock liked the idea. He wasn't sure if he could go through with it, though.

B. I'm slightly uncomfortable with the idea.

How do you feel when you see a same-sex couple in a romantic or sexual situation on screen?

This one was easy.

C. I feel a bit of curiosity or interest.

In your dreams or fantasies, who do you find yourself interested in?

Asher. But he wasn't in the answers. Ever since he'd met Asher, he'd been dreaming about him. He had thought about him often in the days that followed.

B. Mostly people of the opposite gender, but occasionally the same gender.

How do you identify your sexual identity at the moment?

That was obvious. He was on the damned site.

C. Questioning.

Have you ever been attracted to a person regardless of their gender?

B. I'm not sure. It's confusing.

Do you feel your attractions changing over time or depending on the situation?

This situation with Asher was certainly messing with his head. A hint of attraction toward guys had always been there but as more of a curiosity—an admiration.

C. Yes, my attractions can vary.

How open are you to exploring your sexuality further?

Million dollar question. He hadn't meant to flirt with Asher. The words had just dropped out of his mouth. But could he follow them up?

B. I'm a bit hesitant but somewhat open.

Have you ever sought out media that portrays bisexuality?

B. I have come across it but didn't actively seek it out.

How do you feel about the term bisexual?

Given his current state, Shaun had no trouble with this one.

C. It seems like it might apply to me.

Do you find the idea of a same-sex relationship appealing?

That had way too many layers. Shaun knew entering into a relationship with a guy would have its rewards. Similar ways of looking at things. Similar interests. Potential matching libido. But the guys on the team would harass him. That alone was enough to give him pause. Plus, he liked women well enough. He'd be happy spending his life with one.

Shaun scrubbed his hand through his hair.

Or would he?

C. Yes, I could imagine being in a same-sex relationship.

Have you ever felt a desire to kiss or be intimate with someone of the same gender?

Shaun's stomach clenched. Yes. And he was downstairs in his bedroom.

D. Yes, absolutely.

If you felt a strong connection with someone, would their gender matter to you?

The last question. And it was loaded. Asher might identify as non-binary. Shaun wasn't sure. If he did, would that make a difference? His heart told him the answer.

C. It wouldn't matter much if there was a strong connection.

Shaun clicked the results button.

67% likelihood you're bisexual.

Not a strong result but a definitive one. He was bisexual and right now, the person he desired most was Asher. The urge to go downstairs and test the theory was strong. But Asher hadn't shown any interest in him. In fact, Asher seemed quite uninterested. He was simply putting up with him.

Shaun retreated from his door and found his way over to his bed. He flopped down on it fully clothed. He'd be bumping around the house tomorrow. He wondered if Asher would be. The other two guys had jobs to go to. The place would be empty for most of the day.

He closed his eyes. Images of kissing Asher drifted into his mind. His lips were soft; his face delicate in his hand. Asher was elevated on his toes to reach his lips.

Sighing and whimpering.

He lifted Asher into his arms and carried him to his bedroom.

He stripped Asher and kissed every piece of his bare skin—worshipped him.

Like he deserved.

Shaun rolled onto his stomach and ground his hard cock into the bedding. He pumped his hips, imagining he was buried deep in Asher's ass.

Asher—mewling and crying his name.

Jeezus.

He spilled in his underwear, creating a continuation of the sticky laundry that had been piling up since the night he met Asher. The guy had created an unprecedented need in him.

And where was that going to take him?

He couldn't be lusting over his roommate. It would make things awkward. He was going to have to get over it. Find a way to put Asher out of his mind.

In the kitchen, the next morning, Shaun found Asher finishing up cooking what looked like oatmeal. It was a lumpy beige concoction sticking to the inside of the pot. Asher dumped the slop into a bowl, set the pot in the sink, and turned on the water to fill it.

Asher jumped a little when he turned and saw Shaun standing there.

"Morning," Shaun said.

"That it is." Asher set his bowl on the kitchen table and curled up on a chair.

The lack of milk Shaun could understand, but Asher hadn't even put any brown sugar on it. He suspected the guy had a thing about maintaining his weight. Shaun hated oatmeal. It had been a staple around his house. Cereal had been too expensive for his family.

His stomach growled as he thought about it. There had been days when he was lucky to get even one meal. Even the oatmeal had been welcome.

"Do you mind if I cook bacon?"

Asher lifted a spoonful of his breakfast. "Don't actually mind the smell of bacon."

"That's because it's *bacon*. What's not to love?"

"That it comes from a pig. An animal more intelligent than a dog." Asher set his spoon in his bowl. "An animal that can be house trained and makes an excellent pet that loves to cuddle."

Shaun scowled. "Okay … you've turned me off bacon … for today."

Asher smiled. "Then my work is done for the morning."

Shaun opened the fridge. "I'm having scrambled eggs. Please don't fill me in on the plight of laying chickens. I know it's bad. The cramped cages and everything. I always buy free-range eggs. At least they get to run around in the sun and eat bugs. Best I can do."

"At least you've thought about it."

Shaun cracked four eggs into a measuring cup and added milk. He took a fork and mixed it all up. He set a pan on the stove and turned on the heat.

Asher appeared behind him at the sink.

"What do you have planned for today?" Shaun asked.

"Groceries."

"You want a ride?"

"I can walk. I don't need much. I'm just short of vegetables mostly."

"I need to go too. I'll walk with you."

There it was again. Suggesting things like they were already friends. It was undeniable that he wanted to spend time with Asher. Burying his attraction to him was going to be hard.

"Okay. Leave in half an hour?" Asher said.

"I'll be ready."

Asher finished washing his dishes, wiped down the counters, and changed out the dishcloth and tea towel. "Is the laundry room in the basement?"

Shaun grinned. "Yeah, but I think it might be haunted down there."

"Noted. Don't linger."

"You can just pitch those in the washing machine. I'll wash some bath towels with them. I think we have a collection of them building up."

"I assure you, you do."

"Sorry. It's a bit messy up there."

Asher simply grunted. A soft, quiet grunt, but a definite sound of agreement. He went to the door to the basement and opened it. He stared down the stairs. "I think you might be right. Definite ghost vibes."

"Run fast. But don't trip on the stairs."

Shaun laughed as Asher thundered down the stairs. The light clicked on. A few seconds. Then the washing machine lid banged closed. Asher ran up the stairs and slammed the door closed.

"Don't like it down there. We should take a vacuum to the rafters and get rid of the spider webs at least. It's creepy like a haunted house. And there is a pile of clothes on top of the dryer."

"Damn. That's mine. Totally forgot about it."

"I can dash back down and throw it all in the dryer. Or does it need to be washed again?"

Shaun scraped the pan with the cooking eggs, shoving them around. It was important not to overcook them. "I'll do it when I'm finished here. But thanks."

"No worries. See you in twenty-five." Asher went to his room and closed the door.

Shaun dumped his eggs onto a plate. He needed to hurry and finish eating. He still needed to get dressed and brush his teeth. It seemed that Asher was exact when it came to time.

He sat at the table. The eggs were perfect.

He pushed his eggs around on the plate. Asher had been on his mind when he woke this morning. He'd *rubbed one out* in bed almost as soon as he opened his eyes. It was becoming a habit. He couldn't stop thinking about him. He was living and breathing thoughts of Asher.

His plate clean, Shaun dumped all his dirty dishes into the sink. He was going to leave them for later. Except Asher had washed his dishes right away. As a roommate, it was the right thing to do; not leave your dishes for someone else to deal with. It was a constant annoyance around the house. Who was in charge of washing the dishes when they all cooked together.

He grabbed the scrubber and the dish soap and went to work. It only took a few minutes. He had plenty of time to get dressed. After brushing his teeth, Shaun slipped on a pair of jeans and a shirt he usually saved for special occasions. He wanted to look good for Asher.

Why, Shaun? Why torture yourself like this?

Because I can't stop myself.

They met in the foyer. Asher donned his massive black coat. Shaun opted for a black parka that would keep him warm for the 15-minute walk to the grocery store.

They started down the sidewalk. The air was crisp; the deciduous trees bare. Evergreens like rhododendrons and cedars provided the only green in the yards they passed by.

"How's school going?" Shaun asked.

"It's my last semester. So I'm thrilled."

"What's your major?"

"English."

"I was never good at English."

"What are you taking?" Asher rolled the reusable bags he'd brought and held them against his chest. "In addition to playing rugby."

"My Master of Education in Coaching Studies."

"That's a thing?"

"I want to get a good coaching position. I need it—it's a thing."

"What else do you do? Any hobbies?"

"I'm pretty busy with school and rugby. I used to run. Don't do it much anymore."

"I've never been in any kind of sports except for the mandatory physical education classes in grade school. I was the one getting pummeled by balls when the teacher wasn't looking."

"Kids can suck sometimes."

"The girls weren't so bad. When they found out I was gay, I suddenly had a flock of them wanting to be my friend. I turned into a commodity to be won over."

"Did you like hanging out with them?"

Asher smiled. "Actually, I did. Playing around with makeup and nail colors was fun." He laughed. "And talking about cute boys. And what we would do with them if we ever dated one."

Shaun laughed.

"Let me guess your favorite nail color—black."

Asher smirked. "How on earth did you know that?"

Shaun nudged him. "You've dropped a few clues. Do you own anything of a different color?"

"I have some dark purple shirts."

"I'd like to see those on you."

Shaun rolled his eyes and stuffed his hands into his pockets. He'd done it again. That had slipped out. *I'd like to see those on you.* He needed to stop doing that. It was the truth, though. Asher's clothes made him look almost exotic. That and the eyeliner and mascara he always wore. He couldn't help but pepper him with compliments. Asher deserved every single one. If Asher hadn't figured out he was attracted to him by now, he was blind and deaf.

Asher didn't answer.

Shaun figured he had overstepped.

They walked into the parking lot of the grocery store.

"Share a cart?" Asher asked.

"Sure. I don't need much. Just some milk and bread."

Asher pulled a cart out of the packed row of them and Shaun followed him to the doors. "Just a warning," Asher said.

"I like to go down every aisle."

"Fine by me."

They headed in the direction of the fruit and vegetables. Asher took his time, looking at the offering of fresh juices lining the aisle off the entry. He selected a carrot juice and put it in the cart. It looked more palatable than the bottles of green stuff. Who knew what was in that?

Next the salads. Asher pulled three bags of a variety of greens from the rack. Shaun grabbed some bananas. He wasn't averse to fruit. It just didn't make up a huge part of his diet. He could mash up bananas and put them on peanut butter toast. Unless Asher was allergic to peanuts.

"You're not allergic to peanuts, are you?" Shaun asked.

"No. Why?"

"I eat a lot of peanut butter."

"Me too."

Asher dug around in his cloth grocery bags and produced some reusable produce bags. Broccoli. Onions. Eggplant. Jalapeno peppers. Garlic. Ginger. And limes hit the cart.

They wheeled past the meat department. Shaun decided to avoid picking up anything from there. It might upset Asher. And that's the last thing he wanted to do.

Asher had spoken the truth. They even went down the aisle with diapers in it. Shaun hung back as Asher strolled down the aisle with canned vegetables. Asher kept his thick blond hair swept off to one side of his head, exposing the clean shaved undercut on the other side. His shoulders were slight. His waist trim. Even with the heavy coat, Shaun could see that. He imagined picking Asher up and tossing him onto his bed. He'd be as light as a feather.

Shaun caught up when Asher turned and looked at him, a quizzical look on his face. Asher didn't say a word. Just picked up two cans of black beans.

Eventually, they made it to the dairy department. Shaun scooped up a 4L container of homogenized milk and a massive block of cheddar cheese. He set it in the bottom basket to keep it separate from Asher's groceries. He wasn't sure how adverse Asher might be to it touching his stuff. Asher grabbed some kind of vegan cheese product.

The bread department was easy. He was surprised Asher wasn't gluten intolerant on top of everything else; he picked up a clamshell of croissants and some tortilla wraps. Shaun scooped two loaves of white bread off the shelf. A package of scones and some cinnamon buns.

He stopped himself from picking up more. The carbohydrate restriction and the fact they were walking this stuff home tempered his hunger for baked goods.

"Self-check?" Shaun suggested.

"No." Asher shook his head. "It's taking a job away from someone."

"You're very conscious of things."

"One life. One world."

"So, we're going to have to up our recycling game at home." Shaun liked saying *home* when it referred to Asher. They shared a space. He'd have plenty of opportunities to be around him.

"I'd appreciate that."

"Done." Shaun unloaded Asher's groceries onto the conveyor belt first. "We have containers for sorting everything around somewhere."

Asher paid for his groceries and filled his bags with them. There was no room for Shaun's stuff. Shaun had forgotten to grab some reusable bags, so he ended up buying two paper bags. They were going to be awkward to walk home with.

They left the grocery store and passed by a liquor store.

"Do you need anything?" Shaun asked.

"I don't drink much. Not at home anyway."

"I don't need to go in. We have plenty of beer at home."

Asher smirked. "Beer guy, huh?"

"Does that fit into the jock stereotype enough for you?" Shaun laughed.

"I never said that."

For the next few minutes, they walked in silence.

"You seeing anyone?" Asher asked.

It surprised Shaun, the question. It bordered on being a pick-up line. But it was just an innocent question. A getting-to-know-your-new roommate type of question.

"No. Haven't dated for months. Too busy."

"Me either. Not dating anyone."

Shaun shifted the grocery bags in his arms. He was right. They were awkward. Asher on the other hand was striding along less encumbered, handles on his bags.

He was happy to hear Asher wasn't seeing anyone. Not that he was going to take a shot. It just comforted him that no one else was curling up with Asher. Cuddling him. Kissing him—being intimate with him. Getting to see what was beneath all of that black clothing.

"It wouldn't be fair to someone. I'd hardly be around," Shaun said. "Wouldn't have much time to spend with them. Plus, there are days, I'm so burned out, I just want to vegetate at home alone."

"I like my alone time too."

They passed the halfway mark.

"Do you ever feel lonely?" Asher asked.

"Yeah … sometimes."

"Nice having roommates?"

Shaun laughed. "Sometimes. Ours are a bit rambunctious."

"Finding that out. I was an only child. I'm used to being alone."

"Six brothers and sisters here. Not sure why my parents had so many kids. They couldn't afford us. I started working at fifteen so I could help out."

Asher stopped and looked at him. "That really sucks."

"Cut my childhood short." They started walking again. "I was happy to help but it was hard. Juggling school, my job, and rugby."

"You played rugby in grade school?"

"That's where I fell in love with it."

"It's nice to be passionate about something."

"It is. Do you have a passion?"

"A few things."

Asher didn't extrapolate. Shaun wasn't sure why. Asher didn't appear to be overly shy. Their conversation had flowed. So far, he was fascinated by the guy.

They clomped into the kitchen and bumped into each other a few times as they put their groceries away. The physical contact fired up Shaun's imagination. The thought of being close to Asher and holding him was turning into an obsession. He wanted it *so* badly.

Asher stored his reusable bags in the back hall.

"I have homework to do," he said.

"Yeah, I've got some writing to get done too."

Asher smiled. "Thanks for coming with me."

"Anytime."

Asher bit his bottom lip. It increased his innocence factor. He looked unsure. Like he was having the same thoughts about them touching each other too.

"See you later," Asher said.

"Yup."

Then Asher was gone. Closed behind his door.

It would be another three days until Shaun saw Asher again. Their schedules kept them from bumping into each other. He was thrilled to see Asher in the kitchen when he showed up there to make dinner. He had a couple of premade chicken cordon bleu that he was salivating over.

"Hey," Shaun said as he entered the kitchen. "Haven't seen you around."

"Yeah. Classes and work. I had to pick up a couple more shifts a week to afford this place. I had a good deal money-wise on my last room."

"Same arrangement? You shared?"

"Three guys. Computer nerds."

"You into computer stuff?"

"I prefer pencil and paper."

"Purest."

Asher laughed. "You have no idea."

Shaun turned on the oven and retrieved his chicken from the fridge. He lined a pan with tin foil and arranged the cordon bleu on it. Asher didn't say a thing about it. He was thankful Asher wasn't one of those vegans who was always in your face about eating meat.

Shaun watched what Asher was making. It seemed fussy. He was making his own burritos. Some black beans were letting off steam in a bowl. Asher would scoop some out, top it with the fake cheese stuff he had bought, and then roll them up like an expert. He appeared to be making enough to last for a couple of days. Shaun had now surmised Asher didn't eat much … ever. He was super slim. Slim and sexy, but sexy in a virtuous way.

Like he had no idea how attractive he was.

Shaun was mesmerized by Asher's small, slender fingers as they went back and forth between the bowl and the tortilla wraps, working efficiently.

To have those fingers on his body ....

Shaun nearly groaned aloud. He had to look away and concentrate on making the salad kit he had pulled out of the fridge. Ceasar with croutons. He mixed it all in a bowl.

Asher finished eating before Shaun's chicken was finished baking. Asher disappeared into his room and Shaun didn't cross paths with him again for another couple of days.

Chapter Five | Asher

Asher set the large cappuccino on the counter. "Sharon?" He smiled at the woman as she approached and picked up her drink. He said *You're welcome* when she said *Thank you.*

He'd been on his feet for 6 hours. There had been a steady stream of customers, most packing the place to get their coffees before work. Now they had the lunch rush happening. In the afternoon, the parent and stroller crowd would show up. It would increase the noise level of the place.

He liked his job well enough. Most customers were friendly and enjoyed a small amount of chatter while they placed their orders. They had regulars. They were fun to talk to. Being an introvert made it difficult to put himself out there every shift. Recharging at home was important.

Drawing and writing were his lifeline.

They were headed for a breather where they could take a few minutes to clean up the mass of dirty dishes and discard the oat, soy, and cow milk containers that had built up.

Asher placed the last drink on the counter.

"Oh, my god." His coworker Angela leaned against the area near the tills. "Thought they'd never stop coming through the door."

"It's good we're busy. Keeps us employed."

"Good way to look at it. Dishes and garbage, or tables and floors?"

"I'll do the tables today." Asher drummed his fingers on the barista machine. "Got something I want to talk about first, though."

Angela rubbed her hands together. "Oh, goody. You got

some gossip?"

"No gossip … just this guy … I think he might be interested."

"Might?"

"He drops the most clumsy compliments. I can't tell if he's flirting with me or he's just trying to be nice."

"What kind of compliments?"

"My outfits—my face—my skirts. Saying he'd like to see me in my purple clothes."

"Hm. Sounds promising."

"He's hard to read until he's looking at me. There's a look in his eyes. I caught him watching me while we were in the grocery store together."

"What kind of a look?"

Asher smirked. "Like he strokes off thinking about me."

"Wow … okay. You get all that from his eyes."

"It's pretty intense—the fire. I don't know what to do."

"Infatuation isn't the same as wanting a relationship." Angela crossed her arms. "Tell me about him. Every little detail you have on him."

Asher sighed. "His name is Shaun and he's one of my roommates."

"Let me stop you right there. Bad idea … but continue."

"He is working on a master's degree and he plays rugby."

"So, he's smart and pretty to look at?"

Asher groaned. "Drool-worthy. He has incredibly broad shoulders. Sculpted biceps and pecs. I'm sure his abs would be lickable. And he's tall. My lips would only reach his throat."

"So far, I like what I'm hearing. What's he like as a person?"

"Oh, that's the best part. Shaun is kind and caring. Gentle. Thoughtful. He's one of the nicest guys I've ever met. He treats me like I'm worth something. Like I deserve to be protected."

"You are worth something. You deserve the best."

"You know I struggle with that."

"I know. So, I'm assuming he's queer."

Asher shook his head. "No. He confirmed he's straight."

"Red light."

"I know. I'm delusional."

"But you think he's interested. Maybe he's not as straight as he thinks."

"I could also be seeing things. Wishing they were true."

"The clumsy flirting, though. I think there's something there but I don't know if you should do anything about it. You might be setting yourself up for heartache."

"I'm so drawn to him. Not sure I can stop myself."

"Then go for it. You might be surprised. He might be all over it."

"I'll think about it." Asher grabbed a clean cloth and some antibacterial spray. He had a lot to think about. If he was wrong about Shaun, and he made a disastrous move on him, living in the same house as him would be more than awkward.

He cleared two tables and deposited the dirty dishes in a bin designated for them. Once he filled the bin, Angela would run the dishes through the dishwasher.

Wiping down all the empty tables gave Asher a few minutes to replay everything Shaun had said or done that he was interpreting as clues of Shaun's attraction to him. Shaun saying he was straight was throwing him off. Why would a straight guy look at him like that?

He lifted his phone out of his apron. He only had another hour to go, and then he had promised his parents he would stop by for a visit. Maybe stay for dinner.

The hour flew by. In part because he was dreading seeing his parents. He talked to his mom every few days on the phone but his dad was a difficult man.

It was a long bus ride to Uplands, the neighborhood filled with people with too much money. His parents' house was the biggest one there. And it was just one of their homes. They had houses and high-end condos all over the world. His childhood had been spent globe-trotting.

His parents had offered to send a town car to pick him up but he had refused. The bus was fine. He arrived close to their house and walked the three blocks and up the driveway.

Asher took a long, deep breath and then let himself in.

"I'm here!" he called out. He hadn't knocked or rung the bell, so the butler hadn't made his way to the immense foyer to meet him. Charles, the butler, strode fast toward him.

"Master Asher. Your parents will be thrilled you're here."

"Come on, Charles. You know my dad doesn't care one way or the other."

"I'm sure I haven't noticed that."

"Liar."

Charles smiled at him. Charles knew damn well his dad was indifferent to him. In his dad's eyes, Asher had already failed in life. Charles had witnessed enough conversations to know that.

"They're just finishing a late lunch in the sunroom. You can join them there or wait for them in the living room. I'll announce that you're here."

"No need. I can find my way around my own house."

"As you wish."

Asher smirked as he removed his coat and handed it to Charles. "You're far too agreeable."

"And good at my job."

"True. Something to be said for that." Asher clapped his hand on Charles' shoulder. "Catch you later when I escape."

"I'll clear the path."

Asher laughed and wandered across the foyer, through the dining room to the kitchen. The glass sunroom was on the far side. It was an addition to the house. The connection between the kitchen and the glass enclosure was also glass. It allowed sunlight to stream onto the countertops and floor. His parents were sitting at a white wrought iron table with a glass top. Asher hated the chairs out there. Even with the cushions on them, they were uncomfortable.

His dad was hiding behind a newspaper.

Asher pulled out a chair. "Mom." He nodded at her. "Dad."

His dad grunted but his mom greeted him.

"Hello, darling. So glad you found time to come see us."

"I've been busy."

"Still working at the coffee shop?"

"Yeah, I like it there." He fiddled with the glass edge of the table. "I moved. The room is more expensive than the last one. I had to pick up extra shifts."

"I don't understand why you don't use your trust fund."

Asher stared at his mom. "You know why."

"Your life would be so much easier."

"I don't want easier. I want real."

"This *is* your real life."

"Not one I want."

Asher's mom sighed. She turned to his dad. "Richard. Anything to input."

"He's made up his mind," Asher's dad said.

"I'm happy, Mom. That's the most important thing."

"Are you dating anyone?"

"No." Asher shook his head. "Haven't met the right person yet."

That was so untrue. Shaun was everything he was looking

for. He was sure of it. He barely knew Shaun but he felt it in his bones. They were compatible in the extreme.

His dad lowered his newspaper. "Dressed like that, you aren't going to find anybody."

"I'll find the right person the way I'm dressed."

His dad grunted and lifted his paper. "No woman is going to want you looking like that."

Asher frowned. "You know damn well I'm not interested in women."

A harumph passed through the newspaper.

"Maybe a woman will come along that *does* interest you," his mom said. "I want grandchildren before I'm no longer around. I'd like to enjoy them for a few years."

"I know."

His parents had been older when Asher was born. Freak unexpected pregnancy when his mom hit perimenopause. They'd been trying to get pregnant ever since they were married with no luck. Moving on in life, they had given up. Then bang—Asher.

His parents were in their 70s.

"Being gay doesn't mean I can't have children," Asher said.

"But they wouldn't be yours would they if you adopted."

"Then I'll use surrogacy and invitro. Make sure my DNA is in there."

"But when?"

"I don't know. I'm not even seeing anyone right now."

His dad chimed in. "You're never seeing anyone."

Asher felt like mentioning Shaun. That there was a guy he thought was interested in him. But he didn't know if that was the actual case yet. He didn't want to jinx it.

"I want it to be the right guy. I'm not going to date just anyone."

"But you want children."

"Yes, Mom. I want children."

A home, children, and an incredible husband. He wanted the whole thing. On his terms. Not reliant on his parents' money. He wanted to achieve it independently with a man he loved by his side. Maybe Shaun was that guy. There was plenty of time to find out.

"Are you staying for dinner," his mom asked. "Cook is making a nut loaf for you."

Asher's stomach growled. He hadn't eaten since breakfast. His usual protein bar lunch had remained in his bag. "Only if we change the subject."

"We can talk about school," his mom suggested.

Asher relaxed. This was a topic he was interested in. His final year had included some intelligent reads. "I have some interesting books to discuss that you might have read already."

His mom smiled. "Okay. Let's do that."

Asher rose from his chair. "Do you mind if I have a nap until dinner? Hang out in my old room for a while." Something was drawing him to visit his childhood.

"Go ahead. There are fresh sheets on the bed in case you want to stay over."

"No. I'm good in my little room at home."

His mom leaned back in her chair. "You said your new roommates are all rugby players?"

"Yeah, they're cool for the most part. One guy doesn't like me but we barely ever run into each other. He works as much as I do."

"It makes me nervous."

"I'm safe, Mom. Don't worry."

"I know you don't want a house but I could buy you a nice condo. Nothing too big."

Asher released a sigh. "Thank you but I'm happy where I am."

His mom flicked her hand at him. "Go on, then. We'll see you at dinner."

Asher nodded and headed back through the kitchen to the hidden staircase in the corner. It was steep and narrow—and dangerous as hell if you were carrying anything.

The staircase opened up very near his bedroom door.

He hadn't been in his childhood bedroom in over 7 months. He wondered if his mom had made any changes. Or was it still his room? He opened the door. Everything was the same as it had been the day he walked out and swore he'd never come back. He walked to the bed and sat down.

The bed was king-sized and only took up a fifth of the room. There was a small sitting area at one end near a fireplace. A dressing room at the other. His own extravagant bathroom.

He looked around the room. Even his pink boa was still draped over his floor-length mirror. His makeup mirror still on the desk. All his stuffed animals were crowded onto one of the chairs in the room. He tried to imagine Shaun in his childhood bedroom. What would he think of it?

Asher shuffled up his bed and put his head on some pillows. They smelled of lavender. He missed that, drifting off to sleep with the scent surrounding his senses. He needed to pick up some lavender linen spray to replicate it. He knew that's what they used down in the laundry room.

He closed his eyes. He'd had a long day. And Shaun was on his mind. He wanted to dream about him. He set his intention and let sleep take him.

Chapter Six | Shaun

Friday, Shaun walked into the living room and found Asher sitting there watching a movie alone.

"What are you watching?" Shaun asked.

"A gay romance."

"Oh." Shaun jammed his hands into his jeans pockets. "Any good?"

"I could take it or leave it. The gay characters are amplified. They're not realistic. Nobody acts like that in the queer community. They're portraying them as sex craved."

"Do you want to do something else?"

Asher turned off the television. "Like what?"

"Do you game?" Shaun sat on the sofa and turned the television back on. He picked up a different remote and an option of different games appeared on the screen.

"I've never tried it."

"Never?"

"No. I wasn't allowed as a child. Never picked it up after that."

Shaun's family hadn't had the money for a video game player when he was a kid. He'd become fully immersed while in university in the dorm rooms he had started out in.

"I can teach you an easy one … if you want."

"Better than doing homework. I need a break."

Shaun collected two controllers from a shelf under the coffee table. He chose a simple racing game. Asher should be able to keep his car on the racetrack.

He held a controller in front of Asher.

"These two buttons here are for speed." He touched each

button. "Faster. Slower. This toggle is for steering. You can use it for speed too but that can be tricky for a beginner."

Asher repeated what Shaun had said.

"Got it." Asher looked at the screen. "Which car is mine?"

"The one on the left. Wait for the starting gun."

The starting gun went off and Asher was slow to get started. Shaun took off down the track. Asher soon caught up. He was using the toggle for the whole thing. The guy was a natural.

Asher laughed, took a hard right, and leaned in his car's direction. His shoulder pressed against Shaun's. Asher didn't appear to notice. He kept it there. Even nudged Shaun's arm with his elbow as he overtook Shaun. In the final stretch, Asher lay on the speed and beat Shaun across the finish line. Asher whooped and nearly threw his controller in the air.

Shaun had to smile. The guy could be exuberant when he wanted to be.

"Are you a ringer or something?" Shaun asked.

"No. I've seriously never played a video game before."

"You have the gift."

"Beginners luck." Asher patted Shaun's thigh. "Can we play again?"

The brief contact set off fireworks in Shaun's gut. He'd never reacted to someone like this before. The draw to be near Asher was on a whole different level.

"You guys see my razor?"

Shaun turned to the voice.

Asher made a little squeaking noise.

"Jeezus, Matthew!" Their exhibitionist roommate was standing at the base of the staircase in the nude. "At least put some underwear on."

Asher gripped his knee. Shaun turned to look at him. Asher had covered his eyes with his other hand. His breathing hitched up and down. He was mortified.

"Look what you've done," Shaun said. "You've freaked Asher out."

"Just looking for my razor."

"Swinging your damned cock around. No one wants to see that."

"I have reports to the contrary from the ladies."

"Pfft."

"Have it your way." Matthew mounted the stairs. "I'll keep looking."

Asher patted Shaun's knee. "Is he gone?"

"Yeah. I'll talk to him. He can't keep doing that now that you're here. It's fine with the rest of us. We see him nude all the time in the locker room shower."

"Admission." Asher peered at him. "I've never seen a naked man in the flesh before."

Shaun leaned back as Asher released his knee. Surely, Asher had a long line of people who had spent time in his intimate company. Asher blinked at him.

There was that innocence again.

"You've never dated?" Shaun asked.

Asher shook his head. "Never wanted to with anyone."

"Not even for casual sex?"

Asher wrinkled his brow. "I wouldn't be interested in that."

That statement made Asher even more magical. The innocence and naivety weren't put on. They were truly part of Asher's personality.

"I haven't been as strong that way," Shaun said.

"You've dated a lot?"

"I used to. Sort of. We have a lot of women … fans … that make themselves available."

"Ew."

Shaun laughed. "I know what you mean. I dated a few after sleeping with them. Not a great way to start a relationship."

"Not what I'm looking for."

"What are you looking for?" It was a bold question.

"A solid connection. Mind before body."

Shaun nodded. "I wish I'd had those kinds of convictions from the get-go."

"Not too late to start."

"True." And right now, he felt like he and Asher were making some pretty solid connections. He was feeling closer to him. Like he could trust him with a secret.

Maybe he could.

"I think I might be bisexual," Shaun whispered. Daniel was banging around in the kitchen. There was no way he wanted him to overhear this conversation.

"Really?" Asher angled back away from him. "I never would have suspected that."

"It's a secret."

"I won't tell anyone. How do you know?"

"There have been guys … guys who interested me. Got that twist in my gut."

"Sounds almost definitive."

"Not likely I'll follow through."

"Your friends … your team?"

"Yeah, they wouldn't understand."

"Toxic masculinity."

"Something like that."

Daniel walked into the living room.

"Hey, Shaun, I'm making pasta. Do you want any?"

"No," Asher piped up. "Shaun and I are going for sushi."

That was news to him.

What had brought that on?

"I thought you were vegetarian or something," Daniel said.

"Vegan. And there are plenty of vegan options at a Japanese restaurant."

Daniel grunted and turned his attention to Shaun.

"Are you seriously going out somewhere with him?" Daniel pointed at Asher. "Dressed like that? Are you looking to get your ass beat?"

Shaun looked at Asher. He had on baggy, flowing black pants. A gauzy black shirt and a knubby, dark grey sweater with a hood that he was wearing pulled up over his head.

Shaun thought he looked really good.

He looked at Daniel. "I don't have a problem with what he's wearing."

"Your funeral." Daniel spun back toward the kitchen and left them alone.

"Are we actually going to grab a bite?" Shaun asked Asher.

"Do you want to?"

"Not sure we have a choice."

Asher rose from the sofa. "Then, let's go. I'm starving."

"There's a Japanese restaurant at the top of the block. We can walk."

"Perfect." Asher went to the foyer and slipped on a pair of black and white Chuck Taylors and his long coat. He handed Shaun his parka. "Bundle up. It's nasty out there."

"We could drive."

"No. I need the fresh air."

Asher was right. It was cold and windy and there was a mist blowing through the air. A staple weather pattern for Vancouver Island during the winter.

Thankfully, they arrived in less than 5 minutes.

Shaun scanned the menu. He had no idea what anything was.

"Help," he fake cried and grinned at Asher.

Asher shot him a smile that made Shaun's heart stutter.

"Get something easy. I think you should try a yam roll, a mushroom roll, and a California roll. It just has cooked crab meat in it. And some tempura. Battered and deep-fried veggies and prawns."

"Sounds good." Shaun set his menu down. "What are you having?"

"Some agedashi tofu. Battered and deep-fried tofu. And some edamame which is boiled soy beans with coarse salt. You can try some if you want."

"You not having any fish?"

"No, I've been good about it for the past couple of years. Want to keep that up."

The server came and they placed their order. Shaun was happy that Asher ordered for him. He never would have remembered. Asher asked for some green tea along with his food.

"Do you want a beer?" Asher asked.

"Sure."

Asher ordered a Japanese-sounding beer. Then they were alone again. "So …," Asher said. "Tell me about this possible bisexuality of yours."

Out of left field. Shaun wasn't sure he wanted to talk about it anymore. Especially in public. It was something he preferred whispering to Asher about. But he'd asked.

Asher was obviously interested in hearing more.

"I took an online test," Shaun said.

"Huh. And what prompted that?"

Shaun felt queasy. Asher was digging.

He decided to lie. "It was months back. Just curious, I guess."

"Bi-curious. But you've never acted on it."

"As I said, the guys wouldn't understand."

"You live your life based on what the guys see for you?"

Asher had a point. His life was rugby. And right now, the guys on his team dictated how he steered that life. That's how he ended up sleeping with those female fans.

The guys had cajoled him into it.

He wasn't proud of his behavior.

"For now, I guess. Maybe when I'm out in the real world, it'll be different."

"Bit of advice—don't let anyone else tell you who you are."

Shaun looked across the table. That's exactly how Asher lived his life. Unapologetic. Authentically himself right down to the very last molecule. Shaun frowned, disgusted by how hard Asher's life was by simply being himself. Look how the world repaid him for that.

"I'm not as brave as you."

"Maybe you haven't met the right person."

Maybe I have.

The food was quick to come up. Shaun stared at the assortment of food on a wooden block that had been placed in front of him. A bowl of thin sauce accompanied it.

"Tell me where to start," he said to Asher.

"Try the tempura first." Asher pointed at a pile of fried food. A couple of pieces had prawn tails sticking out from one end. "Dip them in the sauce."

"I don't eat the tails, do I?"

Asher grinned. "No."

While Shaun inhaled the tempura, Asher filled a small bowl with soy sauce and set it on Shaun's board. "For your sushi," Asher said. "Wet one side with it."

Shaun lifted some chopsticks from the table and collected

a roll. He dipped one side in the soy sauce and put it in his mouth. It tasted a little like what he thought the ocean might taste like.

"Seaweed," he guessed.

"Yes." Asher poked at his tofu and used his chopsticks to bring it to his mouth. He nibbled at the edges. Then put the remainder in his mouth.

Shaun looked at the bowl of what looked like pea pods in the middle of the table.

"What do you do with these?"

"Mm." Asher finished feeding himself another piece of tofu. "Best to eat them when they're hot. Pick one up and strip the casing off with your teeth to get at the beans."

Shaun tried it.

Yuck.

Tasted too green.

He made a face that caused Asher to laugh.

"Try the roll that has the pink center. It's the one with crab meat."

Shaun plucked it up with his chopsticks, swirled it in the soy sauce, and popped it into his mouth. Better. "I like that one."

"I like how good you are with chopsticks."

"I'm not a complete heathen."

"Never said you were."

Shaun looked at the board. Along with the sushi, there was a pile of pink shaved something. And a small button of green. "What are these?"

"The pink stuff is pickled ginger. You use it to clear your palette between rolls. You should be able to handle it. The green stuff, though. It'll take your head off if you're not used to it."

"Hot?"

"Very. Hits you right between the eyes."

Shaun dabbed his finger in it. He looked at what he'd collected. Barely anything. He stuck his finger into his mouth. No one had ever accused him of backing away from a challenge.

Bloody hell!

Asher was right. Right between the eyes.

But he liked it.

"Do I touch the sushi onto it?"

"Just a touch. Don't ever let anyone dare you into eating the whole dollop."

"I'll keep that in mind. Not sure I'd find myself here with the guys, though."

"Yeah, I can see them engaging in asinine challenges."

"They're not that bad."

Asher crossed his arms. "Are you saying they wouldn't?"

Shaun grinned. "No, you're right."

Asher picked at the rest of his food. The guy didn't have much of an appetite. Shaun could've eaten the same amount of sushi rolls again. And two more piles of tempura.

"Do you want the rest of this?" Asher pushed his plate of leftover tofu toward Shaun.

"I don't eat tofu … but thanks."

The server placed the check on the table. Shaun snatched it before Asher had a chance to go for it. "I'll catch this one. You can get the next one."

Asher bit his bottom lip. Shaun was distracted by the adorable nature of the response. He knew Asher was thinking. His wheels were turning while he sucked on that lip.

Shaun had implied they'd be doing this again.

Asher was considering what that meant.

The check paid, they bundled up and hit the sidewalk. The wind had grown fiercer. They ended up in a laughing fit as they fought against the gusts. They tumbled into the house winded.

They were slow to leave the foyer. Asher hitched his thumb over his shoulder. "Well, I better get back to my homework. I still have a lot left."

"Yeah. Me too. I'm sure I'm behind on something."

Asher backed away a few steps. "I had fun."

Shaun didn't want him to go. He wanted to head back to the sofa with Asher.

Play games. Watch movies.

Cuddle.

"Me too." Shaun started up the stairs. "Good night."

"Night." Asher smiled at him and ducked through the kitchen doorway.

The next morning when Shaun went down for coffee, he found Asher seated at the kitchen table absorbed in a notebook. He was writing something.

Shaun filled his cup.

He turned to Asher. "Do you want more coffee?"

Asher lifted his gaze and set down his pencil. "Sure. Black." He held out his cup.

Shaun made a point of making sure their fingers didn't touch when he took the cup. He didn't need to fuel his fantasies by knowing what Asher's skin felt like.

He filled Asher's cup, brought it over to the table, set it down, and sat across from him. It was upside down but the notebook had two pages covered in paragraphs.

"What's that?" he asked, sounding more interested than he wanted to let on.

"Just writing something." Asher closed the notebook.

"For school?"

"I might use it for school."

"But that's not what it's for?"

Asher huffed out a sigh. "I write for other reasons too."

"You like writing."

"I'm getting my English degree. Of course, I like writing."

"Oh … Yeah, I guess that tracks."

Asher frowned. "Sorry. I didn't mean to snap at you. I have a lot on my mind."

"I didn't mean to pry."

"No … I know." Asher flipped open his notebook. "I'm writing an essay for a spoken word event I'm going to tonight. I'm almost finished."

"Spoken word. I've heard of that."

It didn't surprise him that Asher had emo-hipster-type interests. He could picture him sitting quietly and listening to someone else speak—getting up and speaking himself.

"Where do you do it?" Shaun asked.

"The coffee shop where I work."

Shaun spun his coffee cup. "And that's … where?"

Asher peered at him from beneath dipped brows. "Café Espresso. Where you rescued me."

"Right." Shaun nodded. "I knew that." The bruise on his cheek and slightly bloodshot eye marring Asher's beautiful face was a reminder of what had happened to him that night.

"Are you still sore?" Shaun asked.

"It's getting easier to breathe."

"Good."

"You?"

"I'm used to being bashed about."

"Rugby is a bit different from getting beat up."

"I would do it again … protect you."

There was a hint of discomfort clouding Asher's eyes. Shaun hadn't meant to make him uncomfortable. He was telling the truth. He would do it again … and again.

Asher didn't respond. Somehow, Asher managed to cross his legs on his chair. He leaned against the table edge and picked up his pencil. He added a sentence to his essay.

"You could come … to the spoken word night tonight … if you want."

Asher looked up at him. His large brown eyes were full of uncertainty. Like he was taking a big risk. Like he believed he'd be laughed at.

"What time?"

"7. After we close to the public."

Shaun had a usual Saturday night planned with the guys after they were home from work. He'd need to come up with an excuse for jamming out.

Tell them you have a date.

That's not what this was, a date. But on the cusp of going for sushi last night, it almost felt like it. They barely knew each other, but this seemed more personal than dinner … Asher asking him to attend an event that would be filled with Asher's friends.

Asher had taken a leap.

He wasn't sure why.

"What's your essay about?"

Asher smirked and Shaun's heart twisted in his chest and left him breathless; that one action of Asher's already burned in his memory. It had haunted him from day one.

"Monsters."

Shaun laughed. "Like Loch Ness?"

"Sort of … but from another world."

"So, you like to write fantasy?"

"Sometimes." Asher tapped his fingers on the page of his notebook. "Other stuff too."

"I read fantasy novels."

Asher's eyebrows shot up. "You do?"

"Does that surprise you?"

A flush rose in Asher's cheeks. It was noticeable against his pale skin.

"A bit."

"Big dumb jock."

"I never said that."

Shaun took a sip of coffee and then set the cup on the table. "I've ventured into shifters recently."

Asher laughed. "Okay … that's really surprising. I read gay wolf shifter stories."

"Never tried those."

Asher tipped his head to one side. "Would you be interested?"

Shaun cleared his throat. "Not sure." Lies. He was going to find some of those later. Load a few onto his e-reader. They would likely include gay sex. He was curious to read about it. He hadn't been brave enough to watch any gay porn since he'd taken an interest in Asher.

Asher opened his notebook. His eyes tracked down the page, then his gaze rose to Shaun's face. "You actually going to come tonight?"

"I'll do my best."

"I'll be working before that. You'll have to find your own way there." Asher lifted his phone. "I have to go soon. My shift starts at noon."

Shaun rose from his chair. "I won't keep you." He pointed toward the kitchen doorway. "Do you need to shower first?"

A vision of Asher in the shower flashed through Shaun's

mind. His cock pulsed and thickened. He was very conscious of the fact he was wearing sweatpants commando. If Asher's gaze lowered away from his face, he'd get an eyeful of Shaun's growing arousal.

"Already had one," Asher replied.

"Good, okay." Shaun turned away from Asher. "I'll have one next." He sped toward the stairs and mounted them two at a time. He needed to turn off his attraction for Asher.

You weren't supposed to lust after a roommate.

It made things messy.

Then why are you going to this spoken word thing?

Maybe he shouldn't. He retrieved some clean clothes from his bedroom and a towel and rushed into the bathroom. He came to a stop and looked around.

What the hell?

The bathroom was spotless. All the towels and dirty washcloths were in the dirty laundry hamper. There were mountains of disinfectant wipes in the garbage beside the toilet. The toilet paper was actually on the dispenser. The mirror was devoid of speckles.

Shaun flicked open the shower curtain. The grout lines of the tiles were clean. He swiped his finger down a row of tiles. They were smooth and clean. The bottom of the tub was the color it was supposed to be. Not dark and grungey. Even the faucet was sparkling clean.

It had to have been Asher. None of the Neanderthals he lived with would consider cleaning the bathroom. Shaun usually had to do it and he hadn't gotten around to it in months.

Shaun cranked the faucet on, diverted the water to the shower head, and stepped into the hot water. He made sure the shower curtain was closed properly. He suspected Asher had cleaned the floor as well. He wasn't going to mess it up by letting water spill onto it.

His cock had softened; stunned by the condition of the bathroom. He felt bad that Asher's first week there had found him scrubbing a bathroom. Even the windowsill had been wiped clean.

Any interest in touching his cock with Asher fixed in his mind disappeared. The only picture he had was of Asher on his hands and knees, washing the floor. It was the least sexy image of Asher Shaun could imagine. He felt horrible that Asher had felt it necessary to clean up after them.

He soaped up his hair with the communal shampoo. Beside it sat two olive green bottles. Shaun lifted one. Conditioner. The brand name, he'd seen before. Not at the local drugstore but in the mall with its own store. The stuff was super expensive. Like he suspected Asher's clothes were.

Shaun finished up his shower. He'd learned so much about Asher in the few minutes he'd been in the bathroom. Even if he was interested in pursuing Asher, he was out of Shaun's league.

Despite the friendship they'd been forming over the past few days.

And how badly Shaun wanted it to turn into more.

Asher deserved the best … and Shaun wasn't that guy.

When he returned to the kitchen to make some food, Asher was gone. Shaun spent the rest of the day gaming in the living room. He always had weekends off work. His job as the assistant rugby coach at the local high school didn't pay well but it kept him afloat.

His day of relaxation was interrupted when Matthew drifted into the house. Daniel was a few minutes behind him. They went straight to the kitchen. The sound of two beers cracking open made its way to Shaun. He set the game controller down and joined them.

"How was your day?" Matthew asked Shaun.

Daniel had disappeared upstairs.

"Quiet." Shaun retrieved a beer from the fridge and opened it. He took a long sip. It was what he needed. He needed a calm mind to sort through his options for the night.

Daniel emerged in the kitchen doorway.

"What the hell happened to the bathroom?"

Shaun cleared his throat. "Asher cleaned it."

"Oh, my god." Daniel laughed. "We have our very own house elf."

Shaun scowled. "Don't call him that."

Daniel looked over his shoulder at Asher's bedroom door. "Why not? He's not here, is he?"

"That's not the point." Shaun shoved Daniel's shoulder. "Don't make me shut you up."

"All right. That's enough." Matthew stepped between them. He glared at Shaun. "I don't know what's gotten into you, but you have to stop threatening Daniel." He turned to Daniel. "And you ... you need to cut out any animosity you have toward Asher. He lives here now."

Daniel grunted and moved away. He leaned against the counter and slugged back his beer, tossed the empty can into the sink, burped, and snatched another one out of the fridge.

"When are we leaving for dinner?" Matthew asked.

Shaun shook his head. "I can't go. Sorry. Something else came up."

"What kind of something?" Daniel asked.

A slow smile spread across Shaun's face. He'd made his decision. He was going to see Asher read the essay he'd been working on. Hopefully, talk with him some more. Sure, the guy was beyond his reach, and the timing was wrong, but he still wanted to be around him.

"I sort of have a date."

"Sort of?"

"I'm just meeting up with someone. Not really an official date."

"Who is she?" Matthew asked. "Anyone we know?"

Shaun smirked. "You know them … but I'm not telling you who."

"Cindy?"

"No." Shaun slipped his tongue across his bottom lip, then trapped his lip with his teeth. Cindy was nice but his mind was solely on Asher. Shaun imagined himself kissing those full, pouty lips of Asher's. Capturing them with the intention of ravaging them.

Not going to happen.

Matthew nudged him. "Where'd you go?"

Shaun laughed. "My mind wandered to finding out what those lips would taste like."

The sound that erupted out of Daniel bordered on devilish scheming. The guy practically had the pick of any girl he wanted and he tended to abuse that. He never stuck with any one woman for more than a week. Love them and leave them was his motto. He was gross about it.

So opposite of what Shaun wanted in his life someday.

He dreamed of having a family. House with a picket fence … a dog and everything.

"Go get her, tiger." Daniel lifted his beer in the air. "I'll be rooting for ya."

"Yeah, yeah." Shaun finished his beer. It was after 6. He needed to get organized so he wasn't late arriving at the coffee shop. He didn't want to miss Asher's essay.

After spending far too much time in his room, he emerged

feeling a little uncomfortable. Both guys needled him about what he was wearing. Shaun had decided against wearing his standard jeans and t-shirt. He didn't want to stand out too much, despite his busted-up face. He'd put on black slacks and a black sweater. He'd even dabbed on cologne.

The cat calls followed him as he left the house. He slid into his ancient Toyota Corolla and drove the short distance to Asher's coffee shop. After he found a parking spot, he sat and stared out the windshield. Being here felt like a step toward something else.

He wondered if Asher would see it that way.

If he didn't, why had Asher asked him to see him speak tonight?

Shaun pinched the bridge of his nose. He was overthinking the whole thing. His roommate had asked him to come to check out something new. That's it.

He spotted Asher as soon as he walked in through the door. He was behind the counter making coffees for the small group of people gathered there. He was laughing and smiling, chatting with the customers while he expertly handled the barista machine.

He looked elegant and gorgeous as he moved back and forth with a confidence Shaun found appealing. He wanted to protect Asher but he also liked that Asher was his own man.

The full force of his attraction to Asher bubbled up into his chest.

He wasn't sure what he was going to do with it.

Shaun looked around the room. There was a chair on its own at one end of the shop, and an assortment of circular tables with three chairs each positioned to face that chair.

He gravitated toward the counter. Asher was the only person here he knew. He'd stick close to him until he knew where he should be sitting.

"Hey," Asher said as he leaned against the counter. "Didn't think you'd come."

Shaun nearly couldn't speak. Asher's soulful brown eyes were defined by black lines. One exotic window peeked out from behind his thick blond hair.

He was smiling.

Asher's lips were slick and glossy and so damn kissable.

Shaun steadied himself. "You asked me to come."

"Didn't think it would be your scene."

"It isn't." Shaun gripped the edge of the counter. He was having trouble regulating his breathing. It was increasing and becoming shallow. He felt light-headed.

"Taking a dive into an unknown?" Asher asked.

On so many levels.

"Something like that."

Asher held his gaze, then rested his elbows on the counter, and leaned forward so he was poised on the surface. He clasped his hands together and lowered his voice.

"You smell good."

Shaun's heart leaped in his chest, wondering if the compliment held any deeper meaning. He'd be lying if he said he hadn't put the cologne on without the intention of attracting Asher's attention.

"Thanks."

Asher moved away. "Do you want a coffee?"

"Just a small one. It's a bit late for me to be caffeinating."

"Room for cream?" Asher lifted a coffee carafe and started to fill a cup. He looked over his shoulder at Shaun. "That's how you took it this morning."

"Yes."

Asher finished pouring and set the coffee in front of Shaun.

He pointed to an old wooden sideboard. "The cream and stuff are over there. Grab a seat. I'll join you in a second."

Shaun was slow to dress his coffee to give Asher time to shut down. His stalling became ridiculously long, so he found a table at the back of the room.

Someone sat in the third chair at the table. The place was filling up. He took off his coat and draped it over the back of the empty chair to save it for Asher.

"Hey, thanks." Asher pulled the chair out and wedged himself into it. It was a tight fit. Asher's thigh came to rest against his. Shaun was sure he felt crackling static building between them.

Asher set his notebook on the table. "Sorry. It's so packed."

"It's fine." Shaun shifted in his seat. His cock had reacted to the contact. He was glad of the dim lighting and the tabletop. The first speaker approached the chair. He tried not to fall asleep as they read a five-minute essay about falling leaves.

The finger-snapping when the speaker finished made Shaun grin. This was a whole different world he'd immersed himself in for the night.

Asher placed a hand on Shaun's shoulder and struggled out of his seat. Without thinking, Shaun placed his hand on Asher's hip to guide him. The temptation was to pull Asher to him.

He applied too much pressure; clung on too tight.

"Excuse me … sorry." Asher squeezed out away from their table and walked to the front of the space. He took a seat and flipped through his notebook.

Shaun held his breath, waiting for Asher to speak. The anticipation of hearing his voice for more than a sentence or two was a welcome escalation after touching him. His heart was running away from him. To touch him—hear him … just be anywhere near him.

"I haven't finished it yet, but picture a post-apocalyptic world," Asher said. "Food is scarce. People are sheltering in burrows. Terrifying creatures are wandering the landscape."

Shaun shuffled forward in his chair. The rest of the coffee shop ceased to exist. The only person who mattered to him was seated on an old wooden chair, knees tucked but sitting up straight. Self-assured. In his element. He was safe and accepted here.

And his voice sounded warm and smooth as heated honey.

"The only thing keeping the creatures at bay is the sound of windmills." Asher folded his notebook in half, exposing the words he was about to speak.

He cleared his throat. "The Wind."

"The soothing serenity of the still silence shouldn't have been there. Glancing over at my baby sister, checking to see if she had stirred. Innocence. Lulled by the drip-drop-drip of rain dancing off the canvas of our makeshift roof. Mother and father had not returned to repair it.

...no hum, no whir.

Burrowing deeper into my sleeping bag, waiting. Drip-drop but no rustle. No rustle, no ruffle—no… the infant beside me squirmed, squinting, arms spread wide.

Hush, Annabelle.

...no hum, no whir.

Sleep, Annabelle.

The depth of darkness seduced her.

Seeping upward into the silence, infusing the absence—icy.

Wrinkling my brow, my mother's caution pierced my senses. Eternal sleep followed silence. Annabelle hadn't even whispered her first words.

...no hum, no whir.

Turning and churning, the whipping of wind, always restless, never satisfied.

Silent."

It took the crowd a second to realize Asher had finished. Then the finger snapping happened. There were murmurs of conversation. Shaun was disappointed there wasn't more to the story. He could have listened to Asher speak for hours. At the front of the coffee shop. In their kitchen.

Lying beside him in bed.

As Asher walked back through the tables, people grasped his wrists as he passed and offered their comments. From Shaun's perspective, it looked positive.

Asher was smiling.

Shaun leaned to one side so Asher could take his seat.

"That was really good."

"Wish I'd finished it but I wanted to have something to read tonight."

"Are you going to finish it?" Shaun couldn't take his eyes off Asher's lips. They made the most incredible shapes when he spoke. He glanced up at Asher's eyes.

"Would you read it if I did?"

Before Shaun had a chance to answer, a new speaker took to the chair and began reading. The room fell silent. This essay was about a day at the beach.

When they were finished, Asher leaned against Shaun. Shoulder to shoulder. Bicep to bicep. Asher was so close that Shaun became immersed in a waft of woodsy aroma from Asher's hair.

"I liked that one," Asher said.

"Lots of great imagery," Shaun replied. He wasn't sure what else to say. The reader had done a fantastic job of taking you to the beach. The sights, the smells, the textures—the emotion.

"I liked the feeling of freedom the words created."

"Like you could go anywhere in the world from there."

Asher placed his hand on Shaun's forearm and Shaun's heart stumbled out of rhythm.

"You were paying attention."

"Trying to."

Asher withdrew his touch for a brief second. "I'm glad you decided to come." His hand landed back on Shaun's arm again. "I know we've just started hanging out. I didn't want it to be weird."

Shaun shook his head. "Not weird."

This time, Asher's hand stayed on his arm. Shaun had the urge to place his hand on top. Asher gripped and shook Shaun's arm. "This guy … you gotta hear this guy."

Then the moment was over. Asher clasped his hands together and bent over the table as if doing so, he'd be able to hear better.

Asher was right. The essay was stunning. A story about struggling with gender identity. It made Shaun think and feel things he'd never known someone might go through. The daily dysphoria of identifying as a gender different than you were assigned at birth. There was a lot of overlap between what was being said about gender and his own sexuality.

Expectations.

He was expected to be straight. By his parents. By his friends—his team. By the world at large as someone who was planning on coaching young people in the sport of rugby.

Shaun crossed his arms. He wasn't straight. He'd never been straight. Hanging out with Asher confirmed that. His mind and body were screaming at him to make a move on the guy.

He wanted Asher to stand again so he could place his hand

on Asher's hip.

Run it down his ass—grasp his thigh.

"What did you think?" Asher asked; his eyes glistening. Shaun wanted to reach up and touch Asher's face. Asher had been close to crying.

"Lots to unpack."

"So much insight." Asher sighed and smiled. "Great way to end the night."

Shaun uncrossed his arms. "That's it?" He'd been hoping to spend more than an hour with Asher. Getting to know each other. "I was just getting into it."

"You can come with me next week … if you'd like."

The small crowd began to shift. Chairs scraped across the floor and tables were bumped as people made their way to the doors. Asher was waiting for an answer.

"If you don't mind being seen with me."

"Wouldn't have invited you if that was a problem." Asher winked at him, then rose to his feet. He pushed away from the table. "You're tolerable."

Shaun laughed. "Tolerable? Great."

"Best I can offer you." Asher tossed a smirk over his shoulder, then headed for an area behind the counter. Asher emerged with a black shoulder bag and the coat he'd been wearing when Shaun rescued him. It brought back vivid flashes of memory from that night.

Shaun touched his injured cheek. It would be a while until he was healed—inside and out. He released a shaky exhale and joined Asher at the door. Once everyone was out, Asher flicked off the remaining lights, stepped outside with Shaun, and locked the door.

"I hope you brought a car," Asher said. "I'm not in the mood for the bus."

"Yeah, but not much of one."

"Wheels and an engine are all I'm asking for."

"I have those." Shaun led the way down the street to where he'd parked his car. He popped open the passenger door and held it until Asher was inside, then closed it.

He was circling past the back of his car when he realized what he'd done. He'd held the door for Asher. He took a moment to collect his thoughts before he climbed into the driver's seat. He had to remind himself this wasn't a date. Shaun started the engine and pulled away from the curb.

Asher gathered his hands in his lap on top of his bag.

"That was a good night," he said.

"It was."

"You weren't bored?"

"Just that falling leaves one," Shaun replied.

"It's a recurring theme with her."

"Fan of autumn."

"I guess." Asher stared out the window, then back at Shaun. "So, how often do you play rugby? Do you only have games on a Friday?"

"Sometimes twice a week. Keeps my schedule crazy packed. I have to fit in our university team games with the high school ones."

"You coach high school kids?"

"Assistant coach."

"Is that what you want to do after you finish school?"

"I hope so. If I can find a suitable school."

"Fulfilling?"

"Hoping to bring the joy of the game to more kids."

Shaun caught Asher smiling at him from the corner of his eye.

"I like that," Asher said.

Shaun cruised down street after street. He was annoyed when he pulled up to their house. Both cars were still in the driveway. The guys had stayed home, ruining the rest of his night. He had been hoping for a repeat of their morning in the kitchen. Asher and him. Just hanging out and talking. There was so much more he wanted to know about the guy.

He parked on the street.

"The hooligans are home," Shaun said.

"You weren't expecting them to be?"

"We usually go out on Saturday night."

"We ... as in, you too? Why didn't you go out with them?"

Shaun turned to face Asher. "I wanted to go with you instead tonight."

Asher leaned his head on the headrest and rolled his body toward Shaun; his cheek pressed to the firm fabric. "I'm glad you did. I usually go by myself. It's more fun with someone."

"I had fun." Shaun played with the button on the handbrake, clicking it in and out. "Sometimes the guys can be a bit much to be around."

Asher put his hand on Shaun's, stopping the nervous, incessant noise. Shaun tipped his head against his headrest as he watched Asher's eyes. Asher's hand was cool against his skin. But the intensity of Asher's gaze created incredible heat in his gut.

He felt as though his core might go super nova.

This here—this was a moment.

They were stepping out of the roommate zone.

"You're not like them, are you?" Asher asked as he caressed Shaun's hand.

"Try not to be."

"Let's start there."

Chapter Seven | Asher

It spilled from his mouth like he was some kind of gigolo, versed in flattering, confident talk. Inside Asher was a quivering mess. He had surprised himself by even touching Shaun's hand.

The urge had built inside him like an unstoppable force.

Shaun possessively placing his hand on his hip in the coffee shop when he stood to read his essay … it had messed with his head, but he'd received his answer. Shaun was interested.

Now he'd placed them in an awkward position. He wasn't sure he wanted to go through with this … whatever this was they might be doing. He'd started a boulder rolling.

Back away.

Asher released Shaun's hand. "Let's go in."

Any longer in that car, Asher risked making a more serious move.

He needed time to think about it first.

Asher followed Shaun through the front door and stopped in the foyer. Matthew and Daniel were in the living room. Hollers and profanities filled the whole house. They were gaming but caught the movement of him and Shaun entering the house.

"You weren't gone long," Matthew said to Shaun. "Strike out?"

"No … it went well," Shaun answered while he shed his coat. Asher smiled as he hung his coat up beside Shaun's. Somehow the night had morphed into a bizarre kind of date.

"How come the house elf is with you?" Daniel asked.

Asher turned and scowled at Daniel.

House elf? What the fuck?

Just because I cleaned the damn bathroom?

The embarrassment rose so fast, Asher barely tempered it in time. He clenched his fists as his stomach rolled. Shaun stepped in front of him, blocking his view of the living room.

"I told you not to call him that!" Shaun shouted.

Daniel laughed. "Maybe he'll clean my room next."

"I swear, Daniel … I'm going to pummel you."

Asher grabbed Shaun's arm, stopping him from launching himself at Daniel. This didn't need to escalate. He wanted Shaun to drop it. Go back to being the guy with the kind eyes.

"Leave it be," Asher said to Shaun, his voice low and pleading. He gripped the thick woven knit covering Shaun's bicep. He could feel the muscle flexing beneath his fingertips.

This was going to go one of two ways. How Shaun proceeded was going to decide a lot for Asher. He had no intention of stoking his interest in a guy who used his fists to solve problems.

He felt Shaun relax.

"You're not worth it," Shaun said to Daniel. "I have better things to do."

"Yeah, right. You keep saving him and people are going to talk," Daniel replied.

Shaun crossed his arms. Asher moved his hand to the center of Shaun's back as he peered out from behind him. This could still go sideways. It felt as though he was using Shaun as a shield.

"So," Shaun said. "Talk. Your opinion doesn't matter to me."

"Really?" Daniel tossed his controller onto the sofa. "And

what does your little girlfriend have to say about that?" He rushed at Shaun and hauled him aside, exposing Asher.

Shaun shoved Daniel and pinned him against the wall beneath the staircase.

"Leave him alone. He's not my girlfriend."

"Could have fooled me." Daniel's face twisted into something nasty. "I see the way you look at him. You're into that little faggot."

The slur cut like a knife through Asher's gut. He wanted to run. He *needed* to run. He raced past the two men, flew into his bedroom, slammed the door, and locked it.

He shook as a sob rose in his throat. He crumpled at the foot of his door and curled himself into a ball. He rocked his body as he cried. A lifetime of bullying replayed in his mind.

At first, he didn't hear the rattle of the door handle.

When he did, the sound terrified him. Daniel was coming after him. He'd dispensed with Shaun and he was coming after him to finish him off.

"Asher … open the door."

Shaun.

Asher was still on high alert. He didn't want to risk it and open the door. Daniel might push his way in after Shaun and then his small space of safety would be invaded.

He'd be in danger.

"Asher, please. Open the door. Daniel left."

Shaun must be sitting on the other side of the door. His voice was coming in through the door's edge halfway down. Asher pressed his cheek to the door.

"You're sure," he said.

"Matthew chased him out. He's talking to him outside."

"What if he comes back?"

"We won't let him hurt you."

Asher took a few deep breaths while he flipped through his options. He was tempted to keep himself locked in his room until morning, then head back to his old house and ask if he could sleep on the sofa until he found a new place to live.

Or he could let Shaun in.

"Asher, please. I'll keep you safe."

Those words of assurance from Shaun soothed him; settled his hammering panic-stricken heart. He rose onto his knees and unlocked the door. He shuffled back to let Shaun in.

When he was in, Shaun locked the door behind him.

"Daniel's out of the house. Matthew is kicking him out for good."

Asher looked down at his hands folded in his lap. He'd remained kneeling. The more tucked he was, the safer he felt. "I've upset the whole house. You guys were fine before I got here."

"Not true. I've never felt comfortable with Daniel. He showed his true colors tonight."

Asher looked up at Shaun. "You said you didn't care if he talked?"

Shaun sat on the edge of Asher's bed. "I meant it." He reached beneath Asher's pillow and retrieved Stanley, Asher's childhood stuffy. "Come here." He lay on Asher's bed on his side and extended an arm. "Get in here with me. Let me hold you."

The sight of Shaun lying there waiting for him, offering him a sense of security he could only dream of had Asher's core warming. He rushed to the edge of the bed and rolled into Shaun's arms.

Shaun tugged Asher until Asher's back was pressed to his chest and handed Asher his comfort toy. Asher closed his eyes as Shaun placed a single kiss on the back of his neck.

"I meant it," Shaun repeated. "I don't care who knows."

"Knows what exactly?" Asher needed to hear it. He wanted to know where Shaun's mind was because he knew where his had carried him.

"That you're all I think about," Shaun said. "Ever since we met, I can't get you out of my head." He brushed his hand down Asher's arm. "That I've dreamed of this … holding you."

Those words—they were the right ones. Asher had sensed a connection. Now it was confirmed. He tucked closer into Shaun's embrace. Shaun slung a leg over his.

Being held like this—it was all new to him and it felt so good to be in Shaun's arms. As long as Shaun didn't want to take this any further, Asher could do this forever.

"Will you stay with me?"

"I'm here for you. All night, if you want."

"Just holding me."

"If that's what you want."

Asher turned his head a little to look over his shoulder.

"What if that's all I ever want?"

The silence from Shaun was long. He could feel Shaun's breath on the back of his neck. This could stop whatever this was between them in its tracks.

"I've dreamed of kissing every inch of your bare skin," Shaun whispered at last.

Asher's cock stirred.

Maybe sex wasn't completely off the table.

Someday.

But the truth was …

"I might feel uncomfortable with that."

Shaun kissed the side of his neck. "Why?"

Asher lifted his stuffy to his lips to hide behind. He'd never spoken this truth to anyone before other than his therapist. "I'm not comfortable in my body."

Shaun shifted and rose onto one elbow. "Like that spoken word piece tonight?"

"Exactly like that."

"I'm sorry." Shaun kissed Asher's shoulder. "I can't imagine what that's like."

Asher swallowed. "Two years ago, I started transitioning. Hormones and everything."

"You're a woman?"

Asher shook his head. "No. Settled on non-binary instead. I stopped the hormones. Kept he/him pronouns for simplicity because they fit well enough."

"But you're not comfortable?"

"I've tried to make peace with my body. It's difficult."

Shaun lay back down and buried his face in the hair at the back of Asher's head. He hummed against it as he hugged Asher closer. "I'll be whatever you want me to be, Asher."

Asher laced his fingers with Shaun's on his chest. What Shaun had said—it was a big deal. He might not ever be ready to be intimate with Shaun.

"Are you sure?"

"I just want to be with you."

Someone knocked on the door. Asher jerked and clutched Shaun's hand.

"Everything all right in there?"

It was Matthew's voice.

"We're good," Shaun said.

"Just wanted to say ... for the record ... I don't care," Matthew said.

"Appreciate it," Shaun replied, then laughed. "Now, piss off. We want to be alone."

"Just keep the noise down."

Shaun was still chuckling when he kissed the back of Asher's ear.

He pulled back.

"Do you mind me kissing you?"

Asher squirmed until he faced Shaun. "No. It feels good." He stroked his hand down Shaun's cheek and along his jawline. "It would feel better on my lips, though."

Shaun smiled. He brushed his hand up Asher's spine to the back of his head. Asher focused on Shaun's eyes. This was a big step. Kissing a guy in his bed. Wrapped up in his arms. The kiss he'd shared in the backroom of the coffee shop had been rough and quick.

The anticipation hadn't felt like this.

Shaun brought their lips together and caressed Asher's with his so soft and gentle. Asher whimpered, his emotions filling him. This is what a kiss was supposed to feel like. He deepened the kiss and was surprised when Shaun's tongue snuck between his lips and into his mouth.

Asher placed his hand on Shaun's chest.

He pushed away.

Shaun circled his hand around to cup Asher's face. "Did I do something wrong?" There was so much concern in Shaun's eyes, it had Asher regretting forcing them to stop.

"It feels too fast … what you did."

Shaun stroked Asher's hair. "Then we can slow down."

"I still want you to kiss me. Just not like that … with tongue."

"We'll keep it simple." Shaun pressed his forehead to Asher's. Asher tipped his chin and captured Shaun's lips. This time, there was no invasion by Shaun's tongue.

Shaun's free hand cruised up and down his back, massaging the back of his neck, stroking his spine—keeping a respectable distance from his ass.

Asher moaned against Shaun's lips. His cock was hard, stimulated by the kiss. He knew Shaun's would be too. A part of him wanted to check—feel it for himself.

Shaun was the one to pull away. "We need to stop. My body … it's getting a little too excited. I want to respect your boundaries. Any longer and I'll be grinding up against you."

Asher was reluctant to stop—but Shaun was right.

He needed to consider Shaun's body too. This had to feel unnatural to him. He had a lot of experience with sex. Being denied the full extent of that pleasure would be hard for Shaun.

Asher just needed them to go slow.

Maybe he'd get there.

Shaun rolled onto his back and pulled Asher to him. Asher curled up against him and put his head on Shaun's chest. The rise and fall of Shaun's breathing lulled him to sleep.

Chapter Eight | Shaun

Shaun awoke to pressure on his chest and an arm draped across his stomach. The soft sounds drifting up from Asher meant he was still asleep. He hugged Asher closer and kissed the top of his head. Last night had been strange. He'd never been in bed with someone before and not consummated it at some point. Often more than once.

Instead, they were lying there with all their clothes on.

Asher mumbled against Shaun's chest.

"What time is it?"

"Early. Maybe 8. Do you work today?"

"Noon."

Asher pushed away from Shaun and propped himself on one hip. He ran a hand through the thick mop of blond hair. "I think I have a kink in my neck."

"You passed out on me."

Asher swung his feet onto the floor; his back to Shaun. "Was that all right?"

"I told you I'd be here for you. You sleeping and drooling on me included."

Asher snorted and laughed. "I don't drool." He turned to face Shaun. "Last night … I enjoyed kissing you. Someday … I want to give you more. I know you need more."

It felt as though Asher had no idea he was more than his body. That he had nothing else to offer. Shaun reached for Asher's hand. He squeezed it. "I need *you*. That's all I need."

"That's going to grow old real quick."

Shaun sighed. "Not going to lie. I want to make you feel good. But if that's not going to take the form of anything sexual, I can deal with that."

He shuffled to the edge of the bed. He needed Asher to understand. He took Asher's face in his hands. "I want the person inside your skin. That's who I'm attracted to."

"Are you sure?"

Shaun swooped in and descended on Asher's lips. They were warm and receptive. Asher kissed him back with innocent fervor. He never wanted to be away from those lips again.

But they had to pause to breathe.

"Breakfast," Shaun said. "I think I can make some pancakes vegan."

Asher smiled. "You're going to make me pancakes?"

"Only seems fair after you made my night."

Asher chewed on his bottom lip as Shaun backed toward the door. "I did?"

"I got to hold you. That's huge." Asher didn't look convinced. "Do I need to kiss you again? Make you believe I want to be with you." He swung the door open.

Asher smirked. "I wouldn't say no."

"Pancakes first, then I'll kiss the syrup off your lips." Shaun strode out into the kitchen. Matthew was leaning against the counter. He was grinning.

"You two have a good night?" Matthew looked on the verge of cracking up. "Some pretty sweet talk going on there."

"Shut it," Shaun said and lifted down two coffee cups. "Mind your business." He filled both cups, set them on the kitchen table, and went in search of pancake mix. If it contained powdered milk, he would track down a recipe he could make from scratch. They had flour and stuff.

"Daniel is coming back this afternoon to move his stuff out.

He's staying at a friend's."

"I don't care where he's staying." Shaun looked at the ingredients listed on the bag of pancake mix. No eggs or milk products. "Asher will be at work. I'll make sure I'm out."

"Is this going to affect the team?" Matthew asked Shaun.

"I'll keep things professional if he does." One negative word about Asher, though, and he'd separate Daniel's pretty little head from his body.

Asher emerged from his bedroom in a new outfit. Instead of the floor-length skirt, he wore one that fell just below his knees. Black and forest green, cut like a kilt with a black turtle-neck sweater that appeared to support his head. On his feet, black platform boots with big silver buckles from the arch of his foot to the top of his calves. They added about two inches to his height. The word that sprung to mind was goth-scott.

Shaun smiled. This was the person he was crushing hard on. The one he'd held all night in his arms. The person he saw standing before him was strong and independent. He hoped Asher saw himself that way. He wandered over to Asher, grinning. "You look like you're going on a raid."

"Maybe I am."

"Where's your sword?"

Matthew groaned and left the kitchen. Shaun hadn't meant it that way.

"I prefer a battle ax," Asher replied. "More crushing power."

Shaun laughed and pulled Asher to him. Asher wrapped his arms around Shaun's waist and clung to him. "What would you know about crushing anyone?" Shaun asked.

"Don't need to … I know this guy …."

"You do, do you?"

With the boots, Asher was tall enough to kiss Shaun's chin.

Asher's lips felt heavenly on his skin. In the light of day, in the kitchen, the affection felt different. They'd been quick to step out of the shadows, but he wasn't sure he was ready to leave the house with their truth on display.

"Pancakes?"

Shaun broke from his thoughts. "Right." He gathered a bowl, a wooden spoon, and the cast iron fry pan. It was seasoned with olive oil. Should be fine.

Asher watched him from the kitchen table where he sipped his coffee. He'd brought a new notebook with him. A different colored one. From the far side of the kitchen, Shaun could barely make out boxes with pictures in them. Asher was sketching in the boxes.

"You know how to draw?"

Asher didn't look up. "Since I was a kid."

"Comics?"

"Sort of. Manga."

"That Japanese stuff?"

Asher huffed out a laugh. "Yeah, that Japanese stuff."

Shaun wandered over with a bowl held against his chest while still stirring. He leaned over the table to see what Asher was doing. "Those look really good."

"Thanks. It keeps me entertained."

Shaun looked closer. Two people were immersed in a passionate kiss.

Was that two guys?

"Gay stuff?"

"Yaoi. Boys love."

"So … gay."

Asher looked up and winked at him. "Maybe they're bisexual."

"True." Shaun went back to the other side of the kitchen.

The pan sizzled when he dropped a spatter of water into it. He poured the first pancake.

"Can I show you something?" Asher asked.

"Sure." Shaun poured the rest of the pancakes and went back to the table. Asher had turned the page in his notebook. The images in the boxes caught Shaun by surprise.

Two men embracing, undressing, hard cocks and precum, then grinding—fucking—cumming. Virile and carnal. Those had come from Asher's imagination.

Shaun touched the page and stroked his finger along the edge of a hard cock.

"You think about stuff like this," he said.

"More than I'd like."

Shaun furrowed his brow. "So … it interests you."

"It does." Asher fiddled with his pencil. "I need to explain something."

The pancakes were going to burn. Shaun didn't care. He sat in the chair across from Asher. Whatever Asher was going to tell him, he was ready. They'd already discussed so much.

Color rose in Asher's cheeks. "My cock and I don't get along well." He cleared his throat. "Not that we don't have the occasional *moment* together."

Asher stared into his empty coffee cup. "I'm not averse to doing certain things. I'd just prefer to leave my cock out of it." He looked up. "If we get there someday."

"Certain things?"

Asher turned the notebook, flipped back a few pages, and pressed his finger to a panel. The two characters were facing each other. One straddling the other. Obviously, being penetrated.

Shaun looked up into Asher's eyes.

Nervous apprehension flicked around in Asher's gaze.

Shaun reached across the table and placed his hand on Asher's. It had taken an incredible amount of courage for Asher to show him that drawing. To ask for what he wanted.

"I'm in no hurry to get there," Shaun said. "But I want that with you too."

Asher's shoulders relaxed. "I'm not saying it will happen."

"It doesn't have to."

Asher nodded. "Okay." He looked toward the stove. Shaun followed his gaze. There was smoke coming off the pan. "I hope you made more batter."

Shaun had been distracted all practice. His mind couldn't detach itself from the image of Asher straddling him, rocking his hips as Shaun worked his cock in and out of Asher's ass.

"Shaun. What the fuck?"

A ball hit him in the side of the head.

"Where the hell are you?" Coach was angry. Shaun's successful tackling ratio was way off. And when he did manage to take someone down, it was sloppy. He ran the risk of getting hurt.

He rubbed his head. Damn balls were hard.

"He's daydreaming about his new sissy girlfriend."

Daniel.

Shaun grunted and turned away. He'd promised himself he wouldn't fight with Daniel unless his abuse got really out of control. Then all bets were off.

He jogged across the field. The practice was over. He could go home soon and immerse himself in Asher's unique affection. It was still new between them. Only a week since he first kissed Asher. Shaun was certain he could get his head back in the game in time for the playoffs.

"Ignore him," Matthew said as he patted Shaun's shoulder

on their way to the locker room.

"Trying to."

"He doesn't understand."

"Most people wouldn't. I don't know what Asher sees in me."

"You must be pushing the right buttons or he would have dumped you by now."

Shaun opened the door to the dressing room. "Yeah, I guess."

"There he is," Daniel called and chucked a towel at Shaun. "The lovesick pup."

"Fuck off, Daniel," Matthew said.

Every practice and game, it was the same thing. Daniel taunted him. Challenged him to react, but stopped short of exposing him. It was only a matter of time until Daniel *outed* him.

And then what would he do?

He stripped off his jersey, gear, and shorts and headed for the shower.

The harassment didn't stop. Daniel followed him and stepped under the showerhead on the opposite side of Shaun. The next six showerheads fired up. It was a full house.

"Funny," Daniel said. "Your cock doesn't look any different."

There were a few snickers.

Shaun scrubbed shampoo through his hair. "You're far too interested in my body."

"No, seriously … I thought it might look different after having that mouth on it."

The insinuation repulsed Shaun. Not that he hadn't thought about it, he had, but he knew the act of Asher putting his cock in his mouth might be repugnant to Asher.

Daniel had no business suggesting it.

"Can it, Daniel." Shaun soaped up his body. "What we do is none of your business." He could feel the rage creeping up his spine. And the uneasiness. Daniel was walking the line.

"The team might care," Daniel continued.

"Don't you dare." Matthew marched across the shower enclosure and grabbed Daniel's arm. "Shaun is right. This is none of your business. Or anyone else's."

Shaun sighed. This didn't need to turn into an outright brawl in the shower. "Leave it alone, Matthew. If Daniel is going to spill … he's going to spill."

The constant threats from Daniel were wearing him down. He and Asher were building something special—he could feel it. He couldn't hide what they had forever.

Charlie, the blind-side flanker, turned off his showerhead and wrapped a towel around his waist. "Something you want to tell us, Shaun?"

Just rip the damn bandage off.

"I'm seeing someone," Shaun said.

"About bloody time," Charlie replied. "Who is she?"

Matthew nudged Shaun. "You don't have to do this."

"I want to." Shaun turned and let the water flow over his face. He needed to collect his thoughts. He needed to pick the right words. Asher was important to him.

"You're keeping us in suspense," Charlie said.

"Yeah, Shaun," Daniel chimed in. "Who is this person you're so obsessed with?"

Just spit it out.

He turned to the room.

"Our roommate Asher," Shaun admitted.

"Oh, my god!" Daniel coughed out a laugh. "I was right."

"Hold up." Charlie appeared at Shaun's side.

Shaun shut off his water. "What."

"I thought your new roommate was a guy," Charlie said.

"He's non-binary."

Charlie shook his head. "Semantics. He has a cock, doesn't he?"

Answering that would fall in the category of too much information. Asher wouldn't appreciate him discussing his body with his teammates. After the pancake morning, Asher hadn't spoken about it again. His discomfort with his body. No one else had the right to bring it up in conversation.

"I'm not answering that," Shaun said as he grabbed a towel and strode out of the shower. Daniel was on him like a bloodhound. Charlie was close behind. The rest of the guys filtered out of the shower and pretended to be busy getting dressed, but everyone was listening.

"We need clarification," Daniel said. "He definitely dresses like a girl."

Shaun furrowed his brow. "No, he doesn't."

"Every time I see him, he's in a damn skirt."

"Seriously, Shaun?" Charlie said. "You're dating a guy who dresses like a chick?"

Shaun jammed his hand into his hair. This was getting out of hand. The picture Daniel was painting for the guys was so far off. "He likes kilts. That's it, so drop it."

Asher had an incredible selection of them. All variations of black and a second or third color in a tartan pattern. Then there were his black floor-length woolen skirts. He couldn't imagine a woman wearing one. Especially with the black kick-ass boots Asher paired with them.

The look was very masculine.

"Bottom line," Daniel said. "Shaun's banging a sissy guy. A little fruity faggot."

Oh, no ... you didn't.

Rage surged in Shaun's chest, and blood pounded up through his jugular, turning his face crimson. It was like a bull had taken over.

My Asher.

No one called him that slur. The fury blinded his intention to keep his fists contained. He couldn't stop himself. He flew at Daniel and his fist made contact with Daniel's chin before Daniel had a chance to defend himself. Shaun pulled back and shook his hand.

Fuck that hurts.

Daniel recovered and launched at Shaun. He wrestled Shaun against a row of lockers, grunting and swearing. Dropping the phrase, "Faggot fucker," again and again.

It fueled Shaun's aggression. He wanted to tear Daniel to pieces. Pummel that pretty face of his into oblivion. They both got a couple of good hits in before they were pulled apart by Matthew and one other guy. The men had to fight with them to create some distance between them.

"Enough!" Coach slammed his clipboard against the door frame. "What the hell is going on in here? You two have been at odds for days. I won't have you killing each other."

Shaun struggled out of Matthew's grasp.

"Daniel's being a bigoted asshole. I was trying to shut him up."

"Is this true, Daniel?" Coach hugged the clipboard to his chest. "There's zero tolerance for that kind of nonsense on this team. In this league. You know that."

"He's fucking his roommate," Daniel countered. "It's fucking disgusting."

Coach shoved Daniel in the chest. "This is a warning. Keep it to yourself. What Shaun does in his free time has no bearing on you. I won't have you tearing this team apart."

He pounded his finger against Daniel's collarbone. "You'll be out before that happens."

Daniel shrugged away from Coach and went to his locker. He partially dressed, collected his belongings, and shoved his way past Shaun, knocking him aside.

Shaun grunted but restrained himself. He lifted his towel off the floor and wrapped it back around his waist. Engaging in nude wrestling hadn't been on his agenda today. He wanted to go home. He pulled on his clothes and slung his sports bag over his shoulder.

"See you at home," he said to Matthew.

"Might want to deal with your face first."

Shaun touched his lip and his cheek. They were tender. He ducked into the bathroom and looked in the mirror. His lip was split and he had a new shiner coming up on his cheek.

He wet a paper towel and dabbed his lip to wipe the blood away. There was nothing he could do about the bruise blossoming on his face. He'd be making friends with an ice pack tonight.

It was an uncomfortable drive home. His knuckles were sore. Gripping the steering wheel made them ache. After pulling into the driveway, he crept into the house, discarded his coat and boots, and made his way upstairs.

His bedroom door was ajar. He pushed it open. Asher was curled up against the headboard of his bed, surrounded by pillows, wearing Shaun's varsity t-shirt, notebook in hand, sketching.

He looked fucking adorable.

"Hey," Shaun whispered.

Asher looked up and his mouth dropped open. He set his notebook and pencil down.

"Rough practice?"

"Rough locker room."

"You got in a fight?" Asher crossed his legs, then his arms.

"Daniel was mouthing off."

"You weren't going to let that set you off."

"He *outed* me in the vilest way possible." Shaun sat on the edge of the bed. "And he said stuff about you …."

"I told you, I don't care what people say about me."

"I care."

Asher uncrossed his arms and pulled the sleeves of his sweater over his hands. He looked down as he brought his hands together in his lap.

"He *outed* you?"

"Sort of. I was complicit in the *outing*."

Asher looked up. "You told your team about us?"

"I did. Unfortunately, it ended in me having to beat the crap out of Daniel."

Asher crawled to the end of the bed. He touched Shaun's cheek with two gentle fingertips. "That looks like it hurts. Let me get some ice." He slid off the bed.

Shaun took the few moments Asher was out of the room to dump the dirty laundry from his sports bag in the hamper. He sat on the bed, arranged a pillow behind him, and leaned against the headboard. Asher walked in with a bag of ice wrapped in a tea towel.

Asher climbed onto the bed beside him, put one hand on Shaun's shoulder, flung his leg over Shaun's hips, and straddled him. He placed the ice pack on Shaun's cheek and held it in place.

Shaun wasn't sure what to do with his hands. He settled on placing them on Asher's hips. Asher had arranged himself in an intimate position. Surely, he didn't expect Shaun to ignore that.

He applied firm pressure to Asher's hips. His cock was reacting to Asher's proximity to it. Shaun closed his eyes and tried to enjoy the simple act of Asher caring for him.

"Never thought I'd date a brute," Asher said.

Shaun laughed and smiled. "That's what you think of me?"

Asher lowered the icepack to the bed and brushed his fingers along Shaun's jawline. He touched the stitching split skin on Shaun's cheek he had earned while rescuing Asher.

"I'm not complaining." Asher shuffled back onto Shaun's thighs. Shaun released Asher's hips. Asher lifted Shaun's shirt and peeked beneath it. "Are you hurt anywhere else?"

Shaun swallowed a lump in his throat. "Just from the practice. My ribs."

"Show me."

He was slow to comply, not sure if he had understood Asher fully. He stripped off his shirt over his head and tossed it onto the bed.

Asher's hand flittered across the skin of his ribcage, tracing the extremity of the bruises developing there. "Do they hurt?"

"You get used to it."

Asher looked up at him. "Can I kiss them?"

Jeezus.

His cock stirred.

He needed to be honest. "Not sure I can restrain myself if you do."

"I want to try."

Shaun flung his head back and hissed as Asher placed his lips on a bruise just below his left nipple. A sheet of Asher's hair tickled his skin. The tingle spread. He wasn't sure if he should touch Asher—potentially startle him—make him stop.

He didn't want him to stop.

Asher dropped a kiss lower down. Halfway to his hipbone. Shaun's hand hovered above Asher's head. He desperately wanted to feel Asher's thick hair between his fingers. To grasp it. Cling to it. Have it be the only thing tethering him to the real world.

Asher hummed against his skin. Shaun's heart beat so fast, he thought for sure, Asher would be able to feel it on his lips. He would need to stop him soon.

Asher's hands came to rest on the top of Shaun's jeans at his hips. He hesitated, then bent forward and kissed the button of Shaun's jeans—slow and tentative.

Reality flooded back in like a freight train.

Shaun touched Asher's face.

"What are you doing?"

"I want to make you feel good."

"You are … you don't need to do that." It horrified him to think Asher might be feeling pressured to take things further sexually. That's the last thing he wanted to do to him.

Big brown eyes blinked at him from above his hard cock. There was determination emanating from them. Asher had made up his mind. Shaun couldn't stop himself. He dug his fingers into Asher's hair as Asher lowered his gaze and mouthed the front of his jeans.

The sensation was hot, damp, and achingly slow. Asher ran his lips up and down the outline of Shaun's cock. He enclosed Shaun's shaft as best as he could with the jean barrier.

Mouthing—licking—using his teeth.

When Asher moaned, it nearly sent Shaun off the deep end. It was taking every bit of self-control he had to keep from gripping Asher's head and jamming his cock against his mouth.

Asher lifted his head, panting. His pupils were blown wide.

He launched himself at Shaun's lips. His lips, his chin, his throat—his neck. Asher tucked his face against the side of Shaun's neck. Asher's fingers went to work on Shaun's button and fly.

"I'm just gonna hide out here." Asher kissed Shaun's neck.

Shaun placed his hand on Asher's; the one worming its way beneath the band of Shaun's underwear. "You don't have to do this."

"I want to. I want to make you feel good."

Asher's delicate, cool fingers gripped Shaun's cock. Shaun moved his own hand away. He had to trust that Asher knew himself well enough to decide when he was ready.

Asher's breath was hot on his neck.

Shaun wrapped his arm around Asher and held him while Asher stroked his cock. His pace was gentle and smooth. Breathy kisses from Asher accompanied each stroke.

It was perfect.

Asher was perfect.

Shaun groaned and undulated his hips. Asher kept time with his rhythm.

Then Asher whispered his name.

Shaun grunted and came with the most peaceful orgasm he'd ever had. It rolled through him like a dream. A fantasy scenario guided by Asher's hand.

Asher's grip was firm until Shaun's body stilled, and then Asher struggled away from him. Out of his arms. Off the bed. "I have to go wash my hand."

"Bring back some tissue," Shaun called after him.

Asher appeared back in the doorway after a few minutes. He had a washcloth draped over his hand. He closed the door, crossed the room, and handed it to Shaun.

"Hot washcloth. It's better than tissue."

Shaun took the cloth, peeled open his jeans, and cleaned his cock and his stomach. He threw the washcloth over the edge of the bed. Asher gave him a funny look but didn't say anything.

He rezipped his fly and button.

Asher looked like he needed to talk.

"In my arms or sitting up?" he asked Asher.

"Sitting up."

Asher leaned against the headboard and set his hands on his outstretched legs.

"I've never done that to anyone before," he started. He peered at Shaun. Shaun decided to let Asher talk. "Like I said … I wanted to make you feel good."

A small interjection. "You did."

"You need to understand, though. I don't need anything from you." He reached for Shaun's hand. Shaun took it in his own. "Not yet, at least. I *do* feel things with you."

That needed clarification. "Like what?"

Asher heaved out a sigh. "Desire. Lust. Like I'd be all right with you doing things to me."

"And that's a big step for you?"

"It's new." Asher picked at the blanket. "I touched myself the day after I met you."

Shaun's eyebrows rose. That was quite the admission.

"Like jerked off?"

"That sounds so vulgar … but, yes."

"And it bothered you?"

"Complicated   relationship   with   *you-know-what*, remember."

Shaun placed his other hand on their joined hands. "How *do* I make you feel good?"

Asher leaned against Shaun's shoulder, then cuddled into his arms. "By holding me." He stroked Shaun's stomach, then kissed his chest. "Just hold me."

"What if I hold *and* cherish you?"

He could feel Asher's smile against his chest. "Even better."

Shaun kissed Asher's head.

That he could do.

Chapter Nine | Asher

It was still dark when Asher opened his eyes. He was plastered on Shaun's chest. Since the night he'd told Shaun that to make him feel good, he needed to be held by him, he hadn't returned to his own bedroom other than to access his closet. Shaun had been bugging him to move his clothes, but he wasn't sure exactly how cognisant Shaun was of the size of his wardrobe.

Regardless, it was a sweet sentiment.

That was almost three weeks ago.

Asher rolled off the bed. He needed to pee.

He was annoyed to see a light under the bathroom door. He leaned against the far wall and waited. After far too long, Matthew emerged.

Matthew spotted him in the dimly lit hallway. "Oh, good. I need to speak to you."

"It's like 4 in the morning. Can't it wait?"

"Every time I see you, you're glued to Shaun's side."

"So?"

"So … I need to talk to you alone." Matthew stepped closer to Asher. "You two have become pretty serious." He crossed his arms. "Have you told him about your family? You asked me to keep it quiet when you first moved in. Now, I'm wondering if that's still the case."

"Why? So you can bug me about it in front of him?"

"No. Because it's a big deal." Matthew furrowed his brow. "Not to sound like an overprotective dad, but what are your intentions with Shaun?"

That was a ridiculous question. They were only a month into their relationship. Sure, things had moved fast, but Asher hadn't given what they had any long-term thought.

"You afraid I'm going to corrupt him with wealth?"

"You have access to enough money to buy your own damn island if you felt like you needed to be alone for a while."

"Doesn't mean I want to." Any longer in this conversation Asher ran the risk of wetting himself. They needed to wrap this up. "I pay my own way. I don't need my parents' money."

"Need it or not … someday you're going to end up with it all. Your parents are old. Is Shaun going to fit into that world if you're still together? He's a pretty basic guy."

Asher wrapped his arms around his waist. "Why do you care?"

"I've known Shaun since elementary school. I care."

Shaun had told him about their long-standing relationship. All the trouble he and Matthew had created as teenagers. The staying out late—drinking—skinny dipping in the ocean. How Shaun had stayed at Matthew's often to get away from his parents. How he no longer talked to them.

"I'll tell him. My parents will want to meet him."

"So, you still talk to them."

Asher threw his arms down to his sides. "Of course, I do. We're not estranged."

The truth was, the last call he'd made to his mom hadn't included any information about Shaun's existence. That had been last week. He'd hidden in his old bedroom to make the call.

He was going to tell them. He just wasn't sure how they would react.

"I'll tell Shaun," Asher said to Matthew.

"Tell me what?

Asher spun. Shaun blocked most of the light from coming through their bedroom door. He was in his boxers and rubbing his eyes. "You guys woke me up."

"And this is where I take my leave," Matthew said.

"Thanks a lot." Asher hurried to the bathroom. He peered out at Shaun before he closed and locked the door. "Go back to bed. I'll explain in a minute."

He retreated to the serenity of the bathroom.

As he sat on the toilet, Asher put his face in his hands, elbows supported by his knees. He groaned into his palms. It was bound to come out, eventually.

They'd been together a whole month. Sharing their last names was inevitable. He finished, washed his hands, and headed back to the bedroom. Shaun was awake and sitting up.

He'd turned on a light.

"What is it you're going to tell me? Sounded serious."

"How much did you hear?"

"Something to do with your parents."

There was no easy way to broach this subject. Just telling Shaun his last name was going to explain a lot. "I'm an Eierkuchen. The sole heir Eierkuchen."

Shaun just blinked at him.

He visibly swallowed. "*The* Eierkuchens."

"For my whole life." Asher sat on the bed and scooted close to Shaun. He gripped Shaun's hand. He needed the familiar connection. "It changes nothing for us."

Shaun appeared to come to. "I'm going to be a high school rugby coach." He scowled at Asher. "What are you going to be when you finish school?"

"Probably an English professor. I haven't decided."

"You haven't decided?" Shaun laughed. A short, curt, unfriendly laugh. "It's kind of been decided for you already, hasn't it?" He yanked his hand away from Asher.

"Why are you mad?"

Shaun's eyebrows rose. "Besides you not telling me some pretty important information about you and your life ... nothing."

"I'm telling you now."

"After Matthew threatened to expose you."

"That's not fair. I was going to tell you. I want my parents to meet you."

"Meet your parents? And what would they have to say about me? I grew up poor. I'd fit in as well as a green banana in a ripe passion fruit store."

"You don't have to fit in." Asher waved his hands down his body. "Do you think I fit in?"

"You don't have to. You're their son."

Asher cringed at Shaun's use of the word *son*. Shaun didn't typically mess up like that. He was his parents' *child*. It was an important distinction.

"Child," Asher whispered.

Shaun's features softened. "I'm sorry. I'm upset but I shouldn't have used the wrong word."

Asher slumped toward Shaun. "Do we have to make this a thing? I walked away from that life for a reason. It didn't feel authentic. What you and I have ... it feels real."

Shaun reached for Asher's hand. Asher entwined their fingers and clung on. This man was his beacon. He *had* thought about it. Shaun was the person he wanted to turn to for the rest of his life.

"What happens when you inherit?"

Asher shook his head. "Nothing. Nothing has to happen. They can't make me use the money."

Shaun smiled. "Not even a little vacation or two?"

Shaun was lightening up. Maybe it had just been a shock. It had no bearing on their relationship. He would make a promise to Shaun that he wouldn't get carried away with the money.

But a vacation with Shaun sounded nice.

"Maybe. I have some favorite spots I'd like to show you."

"Where have you been?"

Asher smirked. "Where haven't I been? We have houses all over the globe."

"So, you grew up like seriously rich."

"Obscenely."

"And you don't want it. Any of it."

Asher cuddled up beside Shaun and put his head on Shaun's chest. Their hands were still joined. Like their lives. "I only want you, Shaun."

Shaun sighed and drew Asher closer to him.

"Can I tell *you* something?"

"You're secretly rich too?"

"No." Shaun stroked Asher's face. "I think I'm falling in love with you."

Asher lifted his head. "You are?"

"How could I not?" Shaun smiled at him. "You're intelligent. You're independent. You're fierce and beautiful, and you're crazy talented. *And* you're warm and cozy. You're perfect."

What Shaun said took a second to sink in. Those were a lot of qualities Asher had never associated with himself. And yet, Shaun saw them in him. And he trusted Shaun.

There was one area where he felt he fell short, though.

"Even without the physical stuff?"

After the handjob three weeks back, there had only been a couple of occasions where they'd ventured there again. Shaun seemed content with it. Asher knew Shaun probably took care of his sexual needs in the shower and that made Asher feel guilty.

"We're working on that. I'm willing to wait." Shaun stroked Asher's shoulder "You're worth it. Whatever you decide … I'm not going anywhere."

"I want to get there. That panel in my Yaoi manga I showed you. I want that."

Shaun cupped Asher's face. "How do we get there?"

The answer was, he wasn't sure. He ran his hand across Shaun's chest. He was wearing a white t-shirt like he always did when they were in bed. "Can you take your shirt off?"

"Sure. Um. Okay."

Asher helped Shaun strip his shirt off over his head.

"Now do mine," Asher said. His heart hammered. Shaun had never seen him without his shirt. Before a shower, he wore his old clothes in, and after, he dressed in the bathroom.

"You sure?"

Asher nodded. "I need to feel your skin against mine."

The urge had been there for weeks but he hadn't worked up the courage to ask Shaun. Now that Shaun had told him he was falling in love with him, he knew this man was the one.

His own heart was pulling hard toward him.

Shaun slowly lifted Asher's shirt off over his head. His gaze fell on Asher's chest, then he reached out and touched it. Stroked his hand across Asher's collarbone, then onto his ribs.

"Too boney?" Asher asked.

"God, no." Shaun looked up at him. "You're beautiful."

Asher peered down at his chest. For the longest time, his pecs had retained the breast tissue he had developed because of the hormone therapy. Now he was fairly flat again.

"Can I kiss your chest?" Shaun asked.

Asher sucked in a breath. He wasn't sure how he would react to the sensation. He lay back on the pillows and touched Shaun's face. "Only because it's you."

Shaun descended on Asher's lips. Sweet—slow. Then Shaun hovered above him. His lips traveled to Asher's chin, his cheek, his jawline, then down to his neck.

Asher closed his eyes and moaned as Shaun nibbled and kissed the skin beneath his ear. He ran his hand into Shaun's hair. Shaun moved down to his collarbone, depositing kiss after kiss.

He placed his other hand on Shaun's head. If he didn't like how it felt, he could direct Shaun away from continuing. Shaun kissed the sensitive skin over his sternum. Asher breathed into it.

It felt good.

Shaun's lips brushed to the right and he rubbed his lips back and forth over his nipple. He stopped and looked up at Asher. "This all right?"

Asher's stomach tightened. He couldn't believe he was going to say this.

"Only if you keep going."

Shaun's tongue took a tentative swipe across his nipple. Asher couldn't contain a groan. He tipped his head back and held tight to Shaun's head to keep him in place.

The ache growing in his chest extended itself to his groin. His cock swelled. Shaun sucked Asher's nipple into his mouth, causing Asher to gasp and undulate his hips.

Shaun took it as a sign. He released Asher's nipple and swung his leg over Asher's thighs while staying under the blankets. His ass came to rest on Asher's shins. Shaun clung to the sides of Asher's ribcage. He lowered his mouth onto Asher's other nipple.

Licking—sucking. Brushing his lips against it.

He set a kiss at the top of Asher's belly.

"God, you're perfect," Shaun whispered.

He lifted his head and caught Asher's attention. "You're perfect."

The adoration he heard in Shaun's voice conflicted with everything Asher thought about himself. He didn't feel perfect. The clothes he wore were chosen to cover himself up.

Right now, he felt incredibly exposed.

Looking down at Shaun, Asher wasn't sure what to do next. His body was asking for something different from his mind.

He lowered his hands to his pajama bottoms. He wanted them off.

Desperately.

"Help me with these." Asher made his decision and lifted his ass to pull the bottoms off.

Shaun placed his hand on Asher's stomach. "Are you sure?"

"Just don't touch it with your mouth or your hands."

"Okay. I won't."

Shaun removed himself from straddling Asher and tugged on Asher's pajama bottoms. He slipped them down Asher's legs and off his feet. He'd flung off the covers to do so.

A roll of panic caused one side of Asher's face to go numb. He didn't want to be on display. He sat up and hauled the blankets back over himself. Shaun helped him.

"Sorry," Shaun said as he tucked Asher in. "I wasn't thinking. I wanted to see all of you."

"Not much to see."

Asher was very conscious of the fact Shaun had seen his hard cock. No one else had ever seen it. No one understood his contention with it.

"Not true. Everything about you is beautiful," Shaun said.

"You need to believe me."

"I'm trying."

"I would never lie to you."

"I know." Asher pulled at the front of Shaun's boxers. "I need to feel every bit of your skin on me. I need you to hold me like that. Without these."

Shaun was quick to shimmy his boxers off and push them to the bottom of the bed beneath the sheets. He arranged himself so Asher could snuggle into his arms.

Asher rolled onto Shaun's outstretched arm and kissed Shaun's chest. Shaun wrapped Asher up with his other arm. He kissed Asher's forehead.

Asher had never felt safer.

Shaun was his safe space.

He moved his hips closer. He needed to feel it on his thigh. Asher's breath hitched as he made contact with Shaun's rock-hard cock. It felt firm and heavy against his flesh.

He lowered his hand and encased it with his fingers.

Shaun groaned and clung tighter to him, and rolled fully onto his side.

Asher had a vision of riding Shaun's cock. Seated atop him—rising and falling. He pressed Shaun's length against his thigh. He stroked the hard shaft and rubbed it until Shaun started pumping his hips and digging his fingers into Asher's shoulders.

An impulse stirred in Asher.

He moved his hand from Shaun's cock to his hip. He shifted closer. An explosion of emotion ripped through Asher as his cock touched Shaun's.

Shaun stroked his fingers along Asher's upper arm.

"Please don't do anything you're not comfortable with. Not for me."

"I won't."

Asher disappeared into the crook of Shaun's neck. He kissed and sucked Shaun's skin. The action wound him up even further. He thrust his hips.

Shaun gripped Asher's waist and tugged him closer.

Their cocks created a hard wedge between their bellies. Asher was ready for it—what came next. The characters in his Yaoi manga had engaged in frottage. He had enjoyed drawing it.

Shaun rocked his hips and groaned.

Under his breath, "Fuck."

Shaun's cockhead jammed into Asher's flesh.

Asher hung on tight to Shaun. Only with this man would he do this. He joined Shaun in moving his hips—his ass clenching and unclenching.

Shaun hauled in a long breath. "I'm going to cum. Do you want me to pull away?"

"I don't want any on me."

"Okay." Shaun scrambled and retrieved his boxers from the bottom of the bed. He wrapped his cock in it and pumped hard. Asher watched his face. It fascinated him when Shaun came.

Shaun grunted and convulsed. Thrust after thrust until he was spent. He flopped back on the bed beside him and stared into Asher's eyes.

"You good where you're at?" he asked.

"I'll be fine."

"You don't want to cum?"

"I don't need to."

The confusion was obvious in Shaun's eyes. Shaun simply wanted to make him feel good. Stopping didn't make sense to him. Graphic images flashed through Asher's mind. The night he'd stroked off to the image of Shaun going down on him. The ache in his cock increased.

He kissed Shaun.

He trusted him.

"Be gentle ... and if I tell you to stop ... you have to listen."

"For you, anything."

Shaun moved his hand down past Asher's belly, through the dusty offering of hair, and enclosed his cock in his large hand.

Asher gasped. It was a strange sensation—having someone else holding it. He was able to disconnect from it. He frowned. That's not what this was about. It wasn't a lesson in body mechanics. He needed to fully immerse himself in the experience.

Shaun's strokes were a little too fast.

"Slow down."

He groaned. *There ... right there.* A bubble of emotion erupted in his chest. He felt closer to Shaun than he ever had before. His lust-addled brain was taking him to unexpected places.

Three words were on his lips but he could feel the physical release building.

His cock insisted on preference.

Asher gripped Shaun's arm. With a little quiet grunt, he came. Every shiver as his cock drained returned him to reality. His cock was in the hand of another person.

Embarrassment flushed his cheeks.

He pulled away.

Shaun studied his face, then frowned.

"Are you all right?"

"I'm a little shell-shocked, to be honest."

"That sounds like a bad thing."

"No ... I liked it at the time. But after ... it's after when I have a problem."

Shaun sat up. "Let me wash my hands and I'll be right back. I need to understand."

Asher lay on his back and covered his face as he waited for Shaun. He listened to the toilet flush and the creaking of the floor as Shaun returned. He wasn't sure what to say.

Shaun crawled into bed. "Can I hold you? Will that make it easier?"

Absolutely.

Asher tucked himself into Shaun's embrace. It would make a difference to speak against Shaun's chest rather than make eye contact with him.

"Explain it to me," Shaun said.

"Okay … full story. When I was a kid, I always felt strange about the thing hanging off the front of my body. I knew I needed it to pee, but beyond that, I didn't like the feel of it.

"Then I hit puberty and I was horrified. It grew—and the damn thing had a mind of its own. I started to wear long sweaters and shirts to hide the obvious bulge in my pants. Then I switched to skirts in the last year of high school. I could hide in them. I still hide in them."

Shaun pressed his lips to Asher's head.

"I had no idea that's why you wear them," he murmured against it.

"They're my armor now, but a couple of years ago, I decided I wanted to transition to female. My feminine side was winning out when I started university. I thought I was MTF transgender."

Asher ran his hand over his chest.

"The hormones, though … I didn't like how my breasts felt."

"You had breasts?"

"Barely. More like puffy nipples and pockets over my

pecs."

"That had to be quite the adjustment."

"I tried. Bought myself bralettes to wear but they made me feel uncomfortable. I didn't like the way I looked in them. I grew my hair longer and dressed in women's clothes but it felt wrong."

"So you stopped the hormones."

"It just wasn't for me."

"That's why you identify as non-binary."

"I don't fit anywhere else. But sexually, it's more complicated. I feel gay. I have the body of a guy and I'm attracted to other guys. But the whole gender identity thing rears its head and makes things complicated. Believe me, I *want to* explore my sexual identity with you."

"Then we keep taking things slow."

Asher rolled back and settled his gaze on Shaun's face. "You're very patient with me."

"Every moment I spend with you is special regardless of what we're doing. I'll meet you where you're at. Wherever that is. I promise you, I'll never push you."

The words were back on Asher's lips.

I love you.

It was too soon, though. He wanted to be sure. Sure that Shaun wouldn't abandon him. He couldn't bear to have his heart torn out. They needed to keep building what they had.

"Thank you." That's the best he could offer. He tucked tight against Shaun's nude body. The hair on Shaun's chest felt good against his cheek; his strong arms were protective.

He knew he needed to let go and trust Shaun completely.

Someday.

Chapter Ten | Shaun

That hadn't been the night Shaun had been expecting to happen anytime soon. Asher had sprung forward in their intimacy in a big way. From cuddling with all their clothes on to writhing nude against each other and spilling their seed beneath the sheets.

He'd learned a lot about Asher last night. He'd opened up to him. He better understood why Asher was reluctant to engage in physical contact with a certain part of his body.

Yet, Asher had honored him by allowing him to do so.

That had taken a lot of courage … and trust.

Shaun slowly lifted a spoonful of cereal into his mouth. His mind was floating. Absolute wonderment had descended on him when he woke up naked with Asher in his arms this morning.

Early on, Asher had redressed beneath the covers of the bed. It hadn't bothered him. Shaun had memorized every glorious part of Asher's body before he'd covered himself up last night.

Someone smacked him on the back of the head.

"You're in fucking la-la land." Matthew poured himself a bowl of cereal. "I'm going to go out on a limb here … are you in love with Asher?"

Shaun sighed. "I think so."

Matthew shook his head. "Never saw that coming." He dumped too much milk into his bowl. It splashed onto the counter. "Experimenting—sure. Falling in love? Not a chance."

Shaun looked at the milk on the counter. Asher would be on it in a hot second when he came down after his shower. The kitchen had never been so spotless. Even inside the cupboards. Everything was lined up perfectly. Dishes and utensils that didn't fit into the orderly scheme were put in a cardboard box. A box Shaun had been asked to take to a thrift store. Asher had replaced all of the glasses, coffee cups, and cutlery because they didn't match. The plates and bowls had passed Asher's critique. Shaun had bought a new set before Asher moved in.

The changes annoyed Matthew.

It had endeared Asher to Shaun.

"I'm running late for class." Asher walked into the kitchen. Shaun was surprised to see he was wearing black jeans. They looked good on him. "Please tell me there's coffee."

"Fresh and ready," Matthew replied.

"I'll put it in a to-go cup." Asher flipped open a cupboard and quickly put his hand on the cup he wanted. There were benefits to having organized cupboards.

Asher frowned, grabbed a cloth, and cleaned the spilled milk off the counter. Satisfied with the state of the kitchen—this was when Asher typically dashed out through the door.

This time, he walked over to Shaun.

Asher leaned over and kissed him.

First time ever. Asher had never kissed him in front of Matthew before. Something had shifted last night with their relationship.

"I'll see you later," Asher said. "I'll be home around 4. I don't have to work today."

"I won't be home until 7. Practice."

"Maybe I'll come to watch you."

Shaun's eyebrows arched. "You would do that?"

"I've never seen you play."

"I didn't think you'd be interested."

Asher laughed. "I'm only interested in watching *you* play."

"You know where the campus field is?"

"I can find it."

Asher touched Shaun's face and kissed him again. He moved away, lifted his bag, grabbed his coffee, and opened the door off the kitchen. Asher looked back over his shoulder and smiled.

"Bye."

The words *I love you* danced on Shaun's tongue.

Asher closed the door behind him.

Shaun's spoon clattered into his bowl. He'd forgotten he was holding it. Matthew started laughing and dumped his empty bowl and spoon into the sink.

"You are so sunk," Matthew said. "Lovesick barely covers it."

"What the hell am I going to do?"

"Have you told him?"

"Not yet."

"He has that look in his eyes when he's near you." Matthew patted Shaun on the shoulder. "You'll know when the time is right … but I think he's there as well."

He was left alone in the kitchen to sort through what Matthew had said. He agreed with him. Asher had that look in his eyes. Dreamy and calm like love fueled them.

Maybe tonight after practice, he'd take Asher back to their room and tell him he loved him. That he could see a future with him. That he never wanted to be without him.

If he did that … and Asher loved him back.

Asher would want him to meet his parents.

Shaun shoved his chair back and turned on the water in the

sink. He started on his bowl, then washed Matthew's too. Meeting Asher's parents. What on earth would that look like?

He had no idea what to wear.

Asher would help him with that.

He wouldn't know what to say.

Asher would prompt him. He'd help carry the conversation if it stalled.

He would be nervous as all hell.

Asher would calm him down.

Shaun placed the last of the cutlery in the drying rack. There was no scenario where he'd feel like he'd been stranded alone. Asher would be at his side.

He closed his eyes. He loved every fiber of Asher's being. That was the honest truth. It had rushed up on him and drifted in slowly all at the same time. His heart had been captured on day one but his love had grown deeper each time he learned something new about Asher. Every moment he spent with him resulted in his love becoming more profound.

His body pulsed with it.

He headed for their bedroom. He had some work to do on his master's program. After that, around 3, he had to go to practice. They needed to run through some new plays to combat what Friday's game would throw at them. It was going to be a tough team to beat.

Shaun pulled out the chair from under his desk and opened his computer. He wondered if Asher would show up. It was cold and wet out. Two things Asher hated.

A knock on his door and Matthew poked his head in. "Forgot to tell you, we have a new roommate moving in next week."

"Oh, yeah … what are they like? Have you met them?"

"Briefly … they're trans. A really nice guy. I posted on a

Queer Roommates site."

Shaun's eyebrows rose. "Because of us?"

"I wanted someone 2SLGBTQ+ friendly. Don't need any more strife in this house. You two technically live together. Any roommate we get needs to be all right with that … which reminds me, does Asher still want his room?"

"I don't know." Shaun wasn't sure. They hadn't talked about it. Asher still used his own room like a glorified dressing room. It would save Asher some money, though. "I'll talk to him."

"Perfect. Thanks." Matthew's head disappeared and he closed the door.

That made him feel better, knowing someone from the queer community would be moving in. They didn't need a repeat of Daniel. Asher moving out of his room completely, though? He wasn't sure what Asher would think of that, except Matthew was right—they *were* living together.

He looked around the room. There was a neat stack of Asher's notebooks on the bedside table, the latest book he was reading, and the little bundle of pencils he used.

A few of Asher's coats and chunky studded belts hung on the back of the door.

They'd already done it, but it was a big step—moving in together.

His gaze landed on the bed.

Asher's stuffed animal Stanley sat in front of the pillows on the neat bedding.

Shaun wandered over, picked up the stuffy, held it to his nose, and breathed in. It smelled like the subtle cologne Asher sometimes wore. He sat on the edge of the bed.

Was there an emotion deeper than love?

It felt like it.

Light and desperation burned inside him.

He set Stanley back on the bed and made sure he was sitting up straight. Asher often held the little bear at night while he slept. Less and less over time.

He returned to his computer. He had a lot of work to do. He needed to focus. Pull his thoughts away from Asher. This was his final semester. He was almost finished school.

And then what?

Shaun looked onto the sidelines for the tenth time in the past thirty minutes. Asher still wasn't there. The last he'd heard from him had been via text. Asher had said he was finishing at the library and then he was going to make his way down to the field.

It was after an impressive tackle, where Shaun had brought down one of their best players that the sound of whistling and hooting erupted from the sideline.

He snorted out a laugh and turned to the sound. He hadn't expected Asher would be a loud, vocal spectator. Yet, there he was, jumping up and down along the side of the field.

Shaun jogged over to him.

"You liked that, did you?" Shaun wrapped Asher up in his arms and kissed his head. He was so glad to see him. Asher smiled as he looked up at Shaun.

"Kinda wish you'd tackle me like that."

Shaun laughed. "Really. Well, we'll have to work on that."

"Shaun!" Coach shouted. "Get your ass back here!"

Asher placed his hands on Shaun's chest and gave him a small push. "Off you go. Don't want your coach to hate me. We haven't even been introduced yet."

An exuberant cheerleader *and* he wanted to meet Coach.

Asher was full of surprises.

Shaun ran backward onto the field not taking his attention

off Asher. His hair looked different. He must have got a fresh shave on his undercut. It would be like Velcro. He couldn't wait to run his hands across it. He groaned softly. His hands in Asher's hair—Asher's soft lips on his.

"Shaun!" the coach barked. "Do I need to employ a no-boyfriends on the field rule?" Shaun had nearly walked backward into a group of his teammates. He hadn't been paying attention.

His focus had been solely on Asher's gentle, delicate face.

He looked like an angel.

An angel dressed all in black.

Shaun pulled it together for the rest of the practice. He wanted Asher to be proud of him. Impressed by what the years of playing rugby had turned his body into. What kind of determination and focus he had. The kind of protection he could offer if Asher needed him.

He wanted to be worthy of Asher's love.

If Asher's heart was even his to cherish.

"Good practice." Asher wandered up beside Shaun as he left the field.

"You an expert now?"

"I was judging based on how your coach was reacting to each play." Asher released a small laugh. "Man, can he ever get mad. Not sure how I wouldn't be terrified all the time."

"You get used to him."

As if on cue, Coach approached them.

"You have quite the fan here," Coach said.

"I sure do." Shaun cleared his throat. "Asher, this is Coach Randy." He drifted a loving gaze onto Asher. "Coach, this is Asher—my boyfriend." He put his arm around Asher's shoulders.

"Pleasure to meet you, Asher," Coach said.

"You too. I'm afraid I'm a fan with training wheels. There's a lot to learn."

"You'll get there. I'm sure Shaun can explain it if you're interested."

"Now that I've seen him playing ...." Asher grinned. "The interest has shot up."

"I assume you're coming to the game on Friday?"

"I'll have to move my shift around at work but I'll be there."

Coach extended his hand and Asher shook it. It had gone better than Shaun had expected. Rugby was such a huge part of his life and it seemed like Asher was going to incorporate part of it into his. Coach patted Shaun on the back and headed toward the locker room.

"I have to head in for a minute and grab my stuff," Shaun said. "I can shower at home. I'll be out quicker that way."

"Sure. Shower at home." Asher grabbed Shaun's hand and swung it back and forth as he looked at the ground. He looked up and smiled coyly at Shaun. "Boyfriend?"

Shaun blinked. Had he screwed up—assumed? They lived together. Surely, that was what they were doing. "Did I get that wrong?"

"No." Asher jumped up on his tip-toes and draped his arms around Shaun's neck. "I've just never heard you say it before. I've never had a boyfriend."

"That makes two of us."

"I like the sound of it—boyfriends."

Shaun wrapped Asher up in his arms. "Do I get special privileges... as your boyfriend?"

Asher tipped his head. "Maybe. Kiss me and find out."

Shaun growled and closed his mouth over Asher's. The taste was intoxicating. He backed Asher against the wall of the entrance to the locker room. Asher leaped up and wrapped his legs around Shaun's waist. Shaun clung to Asher's thighs to keep him secured there.

He pinned Asher against the wall with his hips.

He groaned. Asher's cock was hard.

Shaun dove deeper into Asher's desire. Asher's tongue was the first to explore. Asher was devouring him—moaning and sighing, chasing after more.

Asher pulled away, panting, his dark pupils pleading with Shaun's soul. "How soon can we get out of here?" He lowered himself to the ground.

"Give me 3 minutes. I'll tell Coach I have an appointment."

Shaun stole one more kiss and then jogged into the locker room. He wasn't sure what Asher had in mind. But it was lust-fueled. That much he knew for sure.

He burst through the doors of the changeroom in a hurry. His shorts were doing nothing to hide his erection. He didn't care. His boyfriend was waiting for him.

And something intense had erupted in Asher.

He chucked his clothes into his sports bag. He wasn't even going to bother changing. He just wanted to go home, take Asher up to their bedroom, and find out what his boyfriend's desires were stirring up in him. He would do anything. Anything Asher asked him to do.

"What's the hurry?" Matthew asked as he stepped up beside him. He kept his voice low, which Shaun appreciated. He didn't want to advertise what was happening.

"Asher's waiting for me and he's all over me. I need to get home."

"You guys still in the honeymoon phase?"

"Something like that."

"Want me to hold back coming home?"

Shaun zipped his bag closed. "Could you? I'd owe you

one."

"I'll find somewhere to crash for the night. The house is yours."

"Thank you." Shaun pounded Matthew's shoulder. "I really do owe you. One last favor, though. Can you tell Coach I have an appointment? That I couldn't stick around."

"Done." Matthew grinned. "Now, go get him."

Asher had his coat pulled tight around him as Shaun emerged. It had started raining. Asher had taken shelter just inside the tunnel that led to the locker room but his hair was wet.

"Jeez, Asher. You're soaked."

"A torrent came down before I had a chance to duck under cover."

"Let's get you home." Shaun pulled up the collar of Asher's coat to help protect him from the rain and they ran to the car. The whole way home, Asher held his hand.

They walked into a dark house. Shaun flicked on the lights in the kitchen and headed for the stairs. "I need a shower." Asher followed him into the bedroom.

"I'll wait for you here." Asher hung his coat on the back of the bedroom door and sat on the edge of the bed. He fell back and collected Stanley, and held the teddy bear to his throat.

Shaun leaned down, kissed Asher, and patted Stanley's back.

"Be right back."

He was going to shower quickly. Give himself a good scrub-down—but quick.

Shaun immersed himself in the hot spray. Shampooed and half-soaped up, he was startled when the bathroom door popped open.

"Shaun?" Asher's voice was quiet and timid.

Shaun pulled the curtain back far enough to peer out. Asher stood there, staring at him. Shaun's breath quickened as Asher closed the door and began peeling off his clothes.

His sweater and his undershirt first.

His skin was like ivory. His arms and torso lean. He had a habit of not rolling his shoulders far enough back. Like he was trying to protect himself.

Asher unlatched and unzipped his jeans.

The look on his face told a complete story. He wanted this … but he was scared.

"Take your time," Shaun said. "We'll move at your speed."

Asher nodded and shoved his jeans down to his ankles. He stepped out of them, reached down, and picked them and his other clothes up off the floor.

He folded everything and set them on the counter.

Shaun swallowed. Asher was wearing hot pink, lacey panties. The sight made his heart stumble through a few unsteady beats. He hadn't thought he'd be into that.

Asher hooked his thumbs in the thin, side straps.

"Turn around," he said.

Shaun did as he was told. Agonizingly slow moments later, the shower curtain rattled and moved, and Asher's hand came to rest on the small of Shaun's back, pushing him forward.

"You can turn around," Asher said after Shaun moved further into the shower.

When Shaun did, Asher had his hands cupped over his cock. He gathered Asher's hands in his by clinging to Asher's pinky fingers. "I think you're beautiful, Asher."

Asher sighed and let Shaun take hold of his hands fully. They fell away from their protective stance. Shaun's breath caught. Asher was the most gorgeous creature he had ever set eyes on.

Asher wandered closer until his cheek was on Shaun's chest. He wrapped his arms around Shaun's waist. "I want you to make me feel good."

Shaun touched Asher's chin and lifted his face. There was fear and wonderment in Asher's eyes. Shaun wasn't going to mess this up. "Let's start slow."

He lowered his head and took Asher's mouth as tender as he could manage. Asher's hands moved onto his ribcage, then up along his spine. Then gravitated south.

A shiver ran through Shaun as Asher's hands brushed across the globes of his ass. They caressed and swept circles across his skin. Shaun shifted forward.

Asher's hands followed.

A rush of pleasure denied coursed through Shaun as Asher released his mouth. The tender lips landed on Shaun's chest—kissing—sweeping. Shaun groaned and jammed his hand into Asher's hair as Asher sucked his nipple into his mouth. Just the right amount of draw; his tight tongue flicked and circled. He ran his fingers through the hair on Shaun's chest as he teased the hard nubs.

"Asher," Shaun whispered.

Asher looked up at him. So much innocence. So much desire. So much of something Shaun needed to name. The words floated off of Shaun's lips. "I love you."

Asher's chest heaved up and down as he stepped away—not saying a word. It terrified Shaun—the silence. Water beating down on them; the shower sounded loud.

The silence continued.

Asher touched Shaun's face and drew his fingers across Shaun's lips.

"I love you too."

Relief coursed through Shaun. They'd arrived there

together. No waiting for the other person to catch up—or not. Shaun cupped Asher's face and kissed him.

Asher was in love with him—they were in love with each other.

The showerhead spat and the water grew colder by the second.

"Let's get out of here," Asher said; his grip firm on Shaun's hands to keep them on him. Shaun had no intention of letting go of him. They toweled off together. In constant contact.

"I should get dressed," Asher said and started to fuss with his clothes. He got as far as slipping the panties back on. Shaun wasn't going to argue with that.

"No need for the rest. Matthew isn't here. We have the house to ourselves."

Asher chewed at the inside of his cheek. "You're sure."

"Come on." Shaun walked Asher to their bedroom, holding his hands and backing toward the door so he could watch Asher's body move in the dim light.

Ethereal.

He closed their door behind them. Asher walked into his arms. The dance started again. Lips—mouths—hands. Caressing and exploring. Shaun took a chance and swept his hands down Asher's back and onto his ass. Asher trembled in his arms and tipped his hips forward, filling Shaun's cupped hands with his warm flesh. The lace felt incredible beneath his fingertips.

"Touch me," Asher whispered. "Touch me everywhere."

Asher gasped and slung his arms around Shaun's neck as Shaun lifted Asher into his arms and cradled him against his body. He carried Asher over to the bed and laid him out on it.

Shaun started at Asher's lips—tender kisses as he stroked Asher's face. Then he swept his hands down to Asher's throat and across his collarbones to his shoulders.

He released his mouth.

He wanted to see and savor every piece of Asher's body. Every tremble. Every quiver. Every goose bump and raised hair. The shape of his mouth as he fought for breath.

His hands encased Asher's shoulders and trailed down Asher's arms to his hands. Along every finger. Small and talented, creativity flowed from those hands.

He clung to Asher's fingertips then released Asher's hands to lower to his sides. Back to his collarbones, down the center of his ribcage—the flat of his soft belly.

Asher sucked in a breath.

Back up to Asher's pecs, he circled each hard nipple with the point of his index finger.

Tiny hairs stood on end and Asher let out a soft mewl.

Straight down to Asher's left hipbone. Shaun leaned down and sucked on it. Asher writhed beneath his touch and ran his hand into Shaun's hair.

"Shaun," Asher whispered.

It wasn't a call for Shaun's attention.

It was an exhalation.

Shaun brushed one hand down Asher's thigh, over his knee, and along his shin. He crouched down at the end of the bed and took Asher's toes into his mouth. The big black boots had been hiding a secret. The salty flesh was as delicate as the rest of him.

He dragged his fingers up to Asher's other hip bone and stopped. Shaun played with the tight string on the panties. He needed to clarify *everywhere*.

"I want to use my mouth," Shaun said.

Asher's stomach rose and fell. "Okay."

A tingle of excitement went straight to Shaun's cock. The

anticipation was like a drug. He let the buzz surround him. He shimmied the strings of the panties down far enough that Asher's hard cock strained against the material. He ran his nose along Asher's shaft and inhaled the scent of him then brushed his lips across the lace. Asher's compact balls were tucked up tight.

Shaun licked the length of Asher's cock—slowly, taking in every sensation. The room was cool. Quiet other than Asher's breathy moans. Subdued lighting. The scent of soap hung in the air. The rough texture of the lace excited his tongue. He wanted to remember everything.

"Shaun …."

Again, not a request.

This time—a plea.

Shaun tugged the panties down until Asher's cock sprang free. He was slow to drag them the rest of the way down Asher's legs. The anticipation still had him flying high.

He discarded them onto the floor.

He headed back to Asher's lips. He wanted to take a moment to check in with him. He left Asher gasping after a hungry kiss. "Only as far as you want to go," he said.

Asher brushed his fingers through Shaun's hair. "Everywhere … everything."

Everything?

This was monumental in Asher's life. Shaun wanted to make this special for him.

"I love you."

"I love you too."

Shaun kissed his way down the center of Asher's body. Asher's cockhead was tight and glistening with precum. Shaun ran his tongue along the slit to lap it up.

Asher hissed, his stomach clenched, and he grabbed a

handful of Shaun's hair.

"Jeezus, Shaun."

Shaun smiled. "Sorry. Never done this before."

"Maybe start with your hand."

Chapter Eleven | Asher

Sensory overload. That was the only way to explain it. The sensation of Shaun's tongue licking the tip of his cock shot straight up his spine. His body calmed as Shaun moved back to his hips—kissing and sucking. Shaun's hand encased his cock and stroked it.

Asher tipped his head back and rode the wave of desire. The lust for Shaun's body had overwhelmed him on the sideline of the field. Watching Shaun work his muscles and defeat his opponent by crushing him into the ground had made his cock stir. He'd never thought watching someone play rugby could be so erotic. He'd wanted those strong hands all over him.

Moments ago, the tender attention Shaun had bestowed upon him, traveling up and down his body with his hands and lips had set his decision firmly in his heart.

Then there was the admission of love—on both their parts. He'd been afraid to say it first in case he'd been mistaken by the way Shaun looked at him. He'd been sure he was watching love grow in Shaun's expressive eyes. He stroked his hand through Shaun's hair.

He wanted this.

With Shaun.

Shaun nudged Asher's shaft with his nose then licked a long line up it. Tingles of exhilaration flooded Asher's body. Shaun encircled his cock with his thumb and finger and pressed the base of his shaft against his body. He was slow as he slipped

Asher's cock into his mouth.

Asher gripped the bedding and clenched his teeth. If he'd thought the earlier exhilaration had been the height of the experience, he was off by a thousand miles.

Shaun sucked and licked, bobbing up and down. Making the most incredible noises. Shaun had been hungering for this kind of contact. Shaun released Asher's cock and sucked one of his balls into his mouth. Warm and wet—circling—sucking while pumping his cock.

Asher was going to cum. He didn't want to yet.

"Shaun."

This time it was a request to stop.

Shaun looked up at him, his face buried deep. "Do you want me to stop?"

"I need something else from you … the manga panel."

Shaun's pupils widened. "Now … tonight."

Asher sat up and stroked Shaun's face. "Yes, tonight. Is that all right?"

"More than all right." Shaun furrowed his brow. "I have lube but I don't have condoms. I didn't think we'd get here for a while yet or ever. I would have picked some up."

Asher shook his head. "I don't want condoms."

The fire in Shaun's eyes was evident. This was more than okay with him. Shaun climbed off the bed and conducted a search of his bedside drawer.

"I had a night with a fan eight months back," Shaun said. "She'd slept with some of the other guys. I decided to get tested a few weeks later. Negative. And I haven't been with anyone since."

"I knew you wouldn't agree if you thought you might be putting me in danger."

Shaun peered at him. "You know I would never."

"I know. I trust you." Asher sucked in a breath. "I want to feel all of you."

"God, Asher, I want that too."

Shaun tossed a bottle of lube onto the bed. Asher touched it. They were really doing this. Fulfilling his manga fantasy. "Where do you want me?" Shaun asked.

"Might be easiest if you lean against the headboard." Asher pulled the pillows away and tossed them onto the floor. Shaun arranged himself at the head of the bed.

Asher's gaze wandered up and down Shaun's body. He was strong and muscular. Broad chest and shoulders. Cut abs. His long, thick cock towered against his belly.

He wanted it inside him.

He straddled Shaun's hips and placed his hands on Shaun's shoulders. Shaun shifted his legs open slightly. Asher kept his cock at the height of Shaun's belly, not sitting on Shaun's thighs. He held Shaun's face, leaned down, and kissed him. He slipped his tongue into the warmth.

They hummed against each other. In sync—completing each other. Asher could feel Shaun fiddling with the bottle of lube beside them with one hand.

"Just a sec." Shaun brought the bottle to his chest and poured out a generous dollop into one hand. He tossed the bottle aside and distributed some of the lube to the other hand.

He reached around to Asher's ass.

Asher closed his eyes and dove back into Shaun's mouth as Shaun's fingers found the edge of his hole. His stomach clenched and he moaned, filling Shaun's mouth with sound.

Shaun breached his hole with one finger, caressing it inside. He pushed it all the way in. It swept past the gland Asher knew was buried there. He shuddered. Shaun's other hand found its way to join the first. More fingers stroked his hole. Asher grunted and pushed back when Shaun slid another finger into his hole. He wanted it all. Right up to the last knuckle.

He was stunned by a slight burn when Shaun pried him open. In and out—wider and wider. Shaun's fingers slipped past the loosening ring of muscle, popping out each time he removed them. The lube felt warm. Shaun's fingers felt even better. He wanted to keep riding them.

"I think you're ready," Shaun said as he slid his fingers free. He clung to Asher's ass. "Let's move to the center of the bed. I want to recreate that picture you drew exactly."

Asher removed himself from Shaun's lap in silence. It was like a dream playing out in slow motion. Shaun moved to the center of the bed. He brought the lube with him.

"Do you want to do this? Lube me up." Shaun held the bottle out to Asher and stroked his cock with his other hand. Asher smirked.

"No. I want to watch you do it."

Shaun held the bottle high over his cock and drooled lube down onto it. "You like to watch me touch myself?" He slid his hand along his shaft distributing the slick liquid.

Asher licked his bottom lip—a slow dash of pink tongue. "I do."

Shaun smiled and coated his shaft and cockhead. "I like you watching me."

Asher straddled Shaun's hips. He took over for Shaun, stroking Shaun's cock. "We can take turns just doing that ... some other time." He moved forward until his cock was pressed against Shaun's abs. Shaun's cock lay against the back of Asher's ass. He ran his sticky hands through Shaun's hair and kissed him. He wanted to capture it. The desire—the anticipation. Shaun took control of his cock and circled it around Asher's hole. He pressed the tip inside.

Asher's heart thundered in his ears—and his spirit spiraled upward.

The invasion was welcome.

He was on the crest of something pivotal in his life. He was going to merge with the man he loved. "Be gentle with me," Asher whispered against Shaun's lips as he held his face.

"Always. You're in control."

Asher lowered himself as Shaun held his cock steady. The heat of the stretch screamed through him. He concentrated on his breathing. He'd known it was going to hurt.

He took his time. There was a clear moment, he felt it to his very core, when his body accepted Shaun's. He groaned and tipped his head back matching the noises Shaun was making.

A tingle stirred in his belly.

He sank as far as he could. There was still a small distance to go but the position prevented it. He needed to move his legs from kneeling to being outstretched behind Shaun—to position them like the panel exactly. He clung to Shaun and shifted. He had to pull away from Shaun's cock. Once he was repositioned, Shaun cupped Asher's ass and guided him back onto his shaft.

The second time was glorious. He wrapped his arms around Shaun's neck and hung on tight. Shaun moved him up and down. Ascending and descending, Asher devoured Shaun's cock.

He looked into Shaun's eyes. They were watching him—profound love and desire spilled from the grey. It was more than Asher had ever dreamed of. Their bodies and souls were joined. Each undulation, Shaun's mouth would open and he'd exhale, soft grunts, intently keeping his gaze on Asher's. They were in their own little world—and it was sublime.

Asher was as close as he could ever be to Shaun. And it almost felt like it wasn't enough. He tipped his head forward and attacked Shaun's mouth. Shaun bent his knees and embraced Asher around his waist. He rocked his hips, drilling higher. Asher thought he was going to pass out.

He hadn't known anything could feel this good.

He wanted more.

Asher caught Shaun's gaze.

"I need you to lie back," he said.

Shaun released him. "Okay." He fell back on the bed and looked up at Asher. Asher struggled back onto his knees, again releasing Shaun's cock from his ass. He placed one hand on Shaun's chest, the other around Shaun's cock. He guided it back inside him.

This time when he sunk onto it, it pierced his insides.

So much higher.

It took his breath away.

"Oh … Shaun … this …."

Shaun looked up at him with such love in his eyes. "You're so beautiful."

This time, Asher believed him. He placed his other hand on Shaun's chest, then both on his belly. He lifted himself up then back down. "Fuck."

He increased his speed, pumping his body up and down, riding Shaun hard. His own cock had recovered after the initial shock of pain. Shaun placed his hands on Asher's thighs and undulated up into him, keeping Asher's pace. The sounds Shaun was making spun a coil in Asher's gut.

His gland became super sensitive.

Oh, God.

Asher's cock pulsed and spilled all over Shaun's stomach. Asher looked down at the mess. He knew what was coming next. His body would soon be filled with Shaun's semen.

He wanted it. That surprised him. He'd initially thought

he'd pull off before Shaun came. Now, he wanted it. Wanted it filling him, leaving a trace of Shaun behind in him.

Shaun grunted. "I'm going to cum. What do you want me to do?"

Asher leaned forward and kissed Shaun. "Fill me, baby," he whispered against Shaun's lips. "I want you to fill me."

Shaun groaned. "Fuck, Asher. I love you." The next few thrusts bordered on violent. Asher was thrilled by them. Then Shaun gripped tight to Asher's ass, jerked, and swore. He alternated between thrusting and stilling. Asher could feel Shaun's cock pulsating inside him.

It was the most wonderful sensation.

Shaun fell still, eyes closed. He opened them and looked up at Asher, still gripping his hips, and smiled. "That was incredible."

Asher smirked. "Better than I thought it would be."

"You're all right?"

"Floating."

Shaun stroked his hands up Asher's back. "Me too."

Asher tipped to one side. "Help me off. My legs are jelly." With Shaun's help, Asher flopped down on the bed beside him. He could feel the wetness between his ass cheeks and thighs.

"I need to go to the bathroom," Asher said. He needed to get most of Shaun's cum out and clean himself. He knew the rest would leak out for a while yet. He'd deal with it when it did.

"Bring back a hot cloth?"

"For sure." Asher rolled off the bed and went to the door. "Are you sure Matthew isn't home?"

"He's staying over at someone's house."

Asher opened the door a crack and peered out. The house was quiet. He dashed for the bathroom. He had never walked around in the nude in his life.

It was a little exhilarating.

The wetness trickled down his leg. He was quick to wet a cloth and wipe it away. A few minutes on the toilet and he'd dispense with the majority of it.

Satisfied, he wet a new cloth with hot water and brought it to the bedroom. Shaun was lying with his eyes closed—his body and soft cock on display.

Asher's cum was drying on Shaun's stomach.

He climbed onto the bed and washed it away. Shaun's hand came to rest on Asher's back as he finished. It felt funny but he didn't want to leave. He tossed the cloth onto the carpet.

"Let me hold you," Shaun said.

Shaun didn't need to ask him twice. Asher tumbled into Shaun's arms. He snuggled up against Shaun's chest, threw an arm over his ribcage, and entwined his legs with Shaun's.

"Matthew asked me something today," Shaun said.

"What?"

"First, our new roommate. He's a transgender guy."

Asher lifted his head. "He did that for us?"

"He wants to make it an inclusive house."

Asher rested his back down. "That makes me happy."

"I knew it would."

"But, what was the question?"

Shaun ran his hand through Asher's hair. "He wants to know if you want to give up your room."

Asher combed his fingers through the hair on Shaun's chest. "That's a big step."

"We're practically living together already. Your most important stuff lives in my room. You sleep in here every night. The only thing missing is your clothes."

"And my commitment."

"Yeah ... that."

Asher's nervous system felt like it was quivering. This was a huge step. Moving in with someone. But Shaun was right. They were practically there already.

"And it'll save you money," Shaun added.

"I don't care about the money."

Negative thoughts infiltrated Asher's mind. What if Shaun broke up with him? He'd have nowhere to go. He might be forced to move back home if he couldn't find a rental.

Was Shaun worth the risk?

One thing would determine that for him.

"Kiss me and I'll make my decision," Asher said.

Shaun turned onto his side and bestowed on him the most loving, intense kiss he'd ever felt from him. Shaun wasn't going anywhere. Asher could feel it in his soul.

Asher broke from the kiss. "I'll move in with you."

Shaun kissed his forehead. "I'll always be here for you. I promise."

"I love you," Asher whispered and brought Shaun's mouth to hover above his.

"I love you too."

Shaun groaned as Asher kissed him, grabbed his ass, and pulled him closer.

They weren't finished for the night.

Chapter Twelve | Shaun

Shaun was right. Asher wanted him to meet his parents. It was Friday, and Asher had booked off work, as promised to watch his rugby game. Afterward, they were going to Asher's childhood home to have dinner with his parents.

Shaun was terrified.

He'd spent some time searching for information on the Eierkuchens on the internet. There was a lot to read. His parents had immigrated from Germany, already loaded with family money, and had set up a computer manufacturing business. One that had taken off. They were making tens of millions of dollars every month. By the looks of the house on the map app Shaun had jumped on after getting the address from Asher, a lot of it likely ended up in their pocket.

Not to mention the multiple homes. Munich, Venice, Paris, Oslo, Singapore, Merida, and Denpasar. And that's just the ones Asher had told him about.

He wasn't sure what he was about to walk into after they left the field.

Shaun managed to stay focused and played a good game. Asher was waiting for him, all grins, as Shaun exited the locker room after the game.

Asher leaped into his arms.

"You looked amazing out there!"

Shaun couldn't help but smile. His boyfriend was proud of him. He wrapped his arms around Asher and gave him a slow, steamy kiss.

Matthew walked by and nudged Shaun's shoulder.

"Find a room."

Shaun laughed. "Later. On our way to Asher's parents for dinner."

"Oooo. Meeting the parents. That's serious. Are you ready for that?"

Shaun clung tighter to Asher. "I love him. I'm ready for anything."

This time it was Matthew who laughed. "Finally told him, huh?"

Asher blinked at Shaun. "You been hanging on to that?"

"Since the first time I kissed you … I've been slowly drowning in love for you."

Matthew made a gagging noise. "This is where I leave." He headed out of the tunnel onto the field and disappeared around the corner.

Asher ran his fingers down Shaun's face. "How long have you been in love with me?"

"Weeks. Deep down, I've known for weeks."

"And you didn't say anything."

"I was scared."

A few more players bumped past them. They offered up a few obnoxious whistles and cat calls but no one said anything negative. For some reason, Daniel hadn't been at the game.

Shaun suspected he'd been kicked off the team.

He hadn't been able to keep his mouth shut about Asher.

Out of respect for Asher, Shaun had refrained from engaging with Daniel with his fists no matter what he said. Asher had asked him to promise.

He'd realized, he would promise Asher anything.

Shaun took Asher's lips again. They'd made love every night since that first time. Sometimes twice. Asher came alive in his arms. Hungry for him. Like this kiss.

It held its own kind of promise.

Just walking up to the front door was intimidating. The house was huge. Not a house … a mansion. It felt weird just barging right in. It hit him full force that this was Asher's former life.

"Hey, Charles." Asher greeted a man in an expensive suit. He was too young to be Asher's father. Asher had told him the story of his surprise conception.

Realization washed him.

My, God. They even have a butler.

"Where are my parents?" Asher asked.

"In the living room waiting for you. Should I announce you?"

"Charles … please. You know the answer to that."

"I'll leave you to it then." Charles gave Asher a slight bow then turned on his heel and left the foyer through a doorway to one side of the impressive staircase.

Asher reached for Shaun's hand and clung to it.

"Let's do this," he said and led Shaun down a short hallway to a wide double doorway. Inside an immense room stretched out. Two people were seated in front of a fireplace at the far end.

Asher nearly had to drag Shaun along, he was so busy looking at the artwork. The room reminded him of rooms he had seen in 1800s period piece dramas. Everything was antique.

"Mom, Dad, we're here."

His mom turned in her seat. His dad didn't. He just took a sip of his drink.

"Come around so we can see you."

Shaun gripped tight to Asher's hand as they rounded the

sofa to stand in front of it.

"So ... this is the boy you've been telling me about."

Shaun swallowed. Asher's mom was looking him up and down.

"Man, Mom. Shaun's a man."

Asher's mom flitted her hand at Asher. "Yes, of course." She sighed and lifted her drink. "He's much taller than you."

Shaun smiled as Asher squeezed his hand. A signal. Asher wouldn't allow this to continue. "God, Mom. Stop objectifying him. He's right here."

"I'm sorry." Asher's mom extended her hand to Shaun. "It's a pleasure to meet you, Shaun. You can call me Carol." She waved her hand at her husband. "This is Richard."

"Nice to meet you both." Shaun cleared his throat. It suddenly felt dry.

"Take a seat," Carol said.

Shaun looked around. There were only two chairs, both near the fire, separated by its expanse. They wouldn't be able to sit together. He wouldn't be able to keep holding Asher's hand.

Asher looked at him. "It'll be fine," he whispered.

Reluctantly, Shaun took a seat.

"Where did you grow up, Shaun?" Carol started.

"In Victoria."

"Sehr gut."

Shaun furrowed his brow and looked at Asher.

"Mom ... English. Shaun doesn't know German."

"Vielleicht sollte er etwas Zeit damit verbringen, eine andere Sprache zu lernen."

"Mom. I'm serious. There's no reason he needs to know another language."

"Alles klar ... all right." Carol sighed and her gaze

wandered over Shaun. "Asher tells me the two of you are in love. Is that true?"

Shaun nodded. "Yes, ma'am."

"Then what happens next? Are you prepared to marry my son?"

"Mom! What are you doing? We haven't thought far ahead."

Shaun looked back and forth between Asher and his mom. His heart was thundering. He *had* thought that far ahead. His gaze landed on Asher. The words were swirling around on his tongue, fighting to be released. He decided to give them their freedom.

"Yes … I want to marry him."

"What?" Asher sprung to his feet. He rushed to Shaun's side and grabbed his arm. "My room … right now." He hauled on Shaun's arm and marched him down the short hallway and up the staircase. Down along another long corridor and into what was supposedly a bedroom.

It had a bed.

"What the hell!" Asher shoved Shaun and sat on the edge of the bed. He crossed his arms. "You going to just blurt it out like that?"

"I'm sorry." Shaun kneeled in front of Asher. "It just spilled out."

"We should have discussed it first. You blindsided me."

"Is it something we could have discussed?"

Asher tipped his head. He frowned. "Of course, it is."

"What would you have said if I brought it up?"

Asher sucked his bottom lip in and chewed on it. Shaun put his hands on Asher's knees. Asher was studying his face. He placed his hands on top of Shaun's and released his lip.

"I would have said yes."

It was as though sunlight tore through his soul and blasted out of him. He felt alight. His heart had never beat so fast. If he could have grinned any wider, his face would have split.

"You would say yes?" He needed to confirm he'd heard Asher correctly.

Asher nodded. Tears rimmed his eyes. "Yes, I'll marry you … you big lug."

"Like soon?"

"As soon as we finish school … we can start our life together." Asher brushed his hand through Shaun's hair. "Home. Family. Children. If that's what you want."

"I want all of that with you."

"We'll do it together."

"Without your parents' money."

"Just us. I'll sell everything off and donate the whole lot."

Shaun smiled. "Can we keep the house in Bali?"

Asher laughed. "As long as you're with me, we can keep any house you want."

"I'm not going anywhere."

"I know." Asher leaned forward and kissed Shaun. He pressed their foreheads together, their lips still touching. "Let's get out of here. All of a sudden, I want to be home." He looked around the room. "This isn't it anymore." Asher kissed Shaun again. "You're my home."

"And you're mine."

Asher was everything Shaun wanted in his life. They were the most unlikely of couples but Shaun didn't care. He loved Asher … and Asher loved him.

He rose and hugged Asher. Asher put his head on Shaun's stomach and wrapped his arms around Shaun's hips. Asher had never clung to him as tight.

"Let's go … and start our life together," Shaun said. "I'm

going to start with your lips."

Dear Reader

I hope you enjoyed reading *Academic Ambition*.

Please take a moment to review this book on the website of the store where you purchased your copy of *Academic Ambition*.

If you would like to touch base and say hello to the author, you can email them at: leigh@leighjarrett.com

About the Author

Leigh Jarrett (she/he) is an unabashedly queer, quirky, and passionate author of Contemporary MM+ Romantic Fiction. Their published contemporary works include warm and always sexy HEA romances as well as dark romances filled with grit, trauma, and angst.

In their hometown of Victoria, BC, Canada, Leigh can be found nestled up with their fabulously supportive wife and trusty laptop or enjoying the wondrous Vancouver Island outdoors.

Please consider subscribing to Leigh's newsletter to stay up to date with their new releases and promos. If you're interested in MM+ Fantasy and Paranormal Romance, check out one of Leigh's other pen names, JT Fader, on their JT Fader Fantasticals website and newsletter jtfadcr.com.

To connect with Leigh Jarrett:

Email: leigh@leighjarrett.com

Website and newsletter: leighjarrett.com

You can also find Leigh on Bluesky

Other Books by Leigh Jarrett

"It all came down to a matter of trust."
A Friends to Lovers M/M Gay Romance
Snowblind

"Find love in the least expected place."
An Enemies to Lovers M/M Gay Romance

Merlot Rebellion

"Risking it all to follow your heart."
A Found Family M/M Bisexual Romance

Capital Adoration

"Brave enough to pursue love."
An Age Gap M/M Gay Romance

Pacific Pursuit

"Recovering true love."
A Second Chance Hurt/Comfort M/M Romance

Drag Undivided

"Strumming your way to love."
A Grumpy/Sunshine Gay Awakening M/M Romance

Rhythmic Bliss